T0209755

ONE FEAR

*An Exciting Story with
Important Evidence*

Jason M. Jolin

WESTBOW
P R E S S°
A DIVISION OF THOMAS NELSON
& ZONDERVAN

WestBow Press books may be ordered through booksellers or by contacting:

WestBow Press
A Division of Thomas Nelson & Zondervan
1663 Liberty Drive
Bloomington, IN 47403
www.westbowpress.com
1 (866) 928-1240

ISBN: 978-1-9736-8133-5 (sc)
ISBN: 978-1-9736-8134-2 (hc)
ISBN: 978-1-9736-8132-8 (e)

Library of Congress Control Number: 2019920165

Print information available on the last page.

WestBow Press rev. date: 12/20/2019

CONTENTS

ACKNOWLEDGMENTS

Thank you to my amazing wife, Kristina Jolin, for reading my book and providing feedback as well as always helping with my questions. I am so fortunate to have you as my wife. I love you and thank you for all your support.

Also, thank you to my pastor of over twenty-five years, Reverend Robert Howard ("Pastor Bob"), for reading my book and providing feedback. I appreciate him as my spiritual shepherd and for providing an opportunity for me to teach at our local church.

Thank you to my parents, Dennis and Deborah Jolin, for their love and support and my parents-in-law, Marcel and Lorraine Laplante, for always treating me like a real member of the family.

Most of all, I want to thank my Lord and Savior, Jesus Christ, for sacrificing Himself to provide a path of salvation for humankind and enabling me to work in the discipline of Christian apologetics.

This book is dedicated to my children—Trevor, Toriana, and Titus. I love you all and am proud of you.

I hope it is helpful to them and anyone else who may benefit from this important information.

INTRODUCTION

What do we fear? *What should we fear?*

Fear is a powerful emotion that impacts all of us. Each of us may have different things that cause us fear (snakes, spiders, flying in a plane, public speaking, etc.), and our degree of fear as well as how we respond to it may be quite different. But everyone experiences fear.

Obviously we have fear because we are afraid of being harmed (or fear for our loved ones being hurt). We recognize a danger. If the danger is immediate, we try to escape or defend ourselves—flight or fight. If it is a potential danger, not yet a reality, we may ignore the possibility or prepare for it.

But are we concerned about the right kind of danger? Let me offer what I believe to be the greatest danger to each and every person—in other words, *what we should fear.*

We are all headed for this danger. Real danger. Severe danger. A danger that is beyond our full understanding. Does it involve physical pain or death? Worse. Much worse. Judgment. A judgment that determines our eternal fate—the destination of our soul. This book is about giving you information to help you avoid this danger. It's a book not just about fear, but also hope. It brings good news.

Perhaps you're not convinced that this danger exists; you might be skeptical that you will face judgment after physical death. Or maybe you feel you already have answers to address this danger. What are the reasons for your current position? Are you open to considering some important information to ensure that you make an informed decision?

The primary purpose of this book is to provide good reasons to believe that our only hope against this danger is true and worthy of our commitment and trust (faith).

Unfortunately, many people live their lives with little concern for this danger. Their time and energy are focused on trying to enjoy life. There's nothing wrong with that, but shouldn't we consider the extreme danger that awaits us? The following illustration will attempt to emphasize this point.

Imagine you are driving a car on a long road trip. You get to determine what course to take as well as most of the stops along the way. Many of the stops are for enjoyment, like going to the zoo or an amusement park. But some stops are necessary to continue the trip, such as refueling or getting food. And some stops are necessary to deal with major problems, such as a flat tire or car accident; you try to avoid these, but some will happen. You believe that your journey will be fairly long, but in reality it could end at any time. You are told that at the end of your journey, whenever that is, you will meet with a judge who will find you guilty of a crime, and the punishment is severe. Very severe. After the verdict, you can make an appeal, but you are not sure it will help, especially if you make the wrong appeal. Here is the big question: Since it's possible this judgment is true and coming at the end, would you spend all your time on the road trip only seeking fun stops, or might you devote some time to researching how to appeal to the judge?

This road trip is an analogy of our lives. We assume that our journey will be fairly long. We hope to live to a normal life expectancy but recognize that something could happen at any time to end our journey. Yes, life is a journey, and although we want to enjoy the ride, we should be prepared for what awaits us at the end.

Let's discuss the illustration a bit further. There are three types of stops in the illustration that correspond to various aspects of our real lives: fun stops are the decisions we make with our time to do things that we prefer to do (e.g., the zoo, amusement parks, going to the movies, vacations, all forms of enjoyment); necessary stops, such as refueling and stopping for food, are decisions we make that are necessary to live life (e.g., get a job, mow the lawn, all forms of work); and major problems that happen during the trip, such as flat tires or car accidents, correspond to painful experiences we encounter in life (e.g., loss of a job, death of a loved one).

All of us have different road trips, some more enjoyable than others, but we are all headed for the same appointment at the end. The judge we will meet is God. The verdict will be against us. We have all broken God's moral standard.[1] Our conscience confirms we are guilty. We all know we have done wrong in life, and doing wrong deserves punishment. As much as we worry about things in life, there is nothing worse than God's judgment and the potential to go to hell forever. We are in danger.

How much consideration do you give this danger? Some people give it serious attention, but many do not. Many dismiss this danger as far off in the distant future. Many are distracted by the joys of this life. Sometimes it takes a near-death encounter, or perhaps the death of a loved one, to remind us of our mortality and consider what might happen after we die. Some refuse to believe that there is anything to worry about; they contend there is no judge, no life after death. Many assume that whatever they desire or prefer regarding religion is true and will remedy the danger. *But it is vital that we understand that our preferences about God and life after death don't influence reality.*

There are many views regarding life after death—about what will happen and how to avoid danger. But since they contradict on fundamental beliefs, they can't all be true.[2] This point is not about being intolerant; rather, it is about being logical about a critical decision we all face.

Is there really a Judge? Evidence seems to be compelling that the Judge exists (more on this later). So what can be done to appeal the judgment? How do you make a decision that determines your eternal destiny? With so much at stake, are you prepared? Fortunately, the Judge is not only holy and just but is also loving and merciful and has provided a way to escape the danger.

This book is about giving you information to make a decision about the oncoming danger. *My intention is not to be disrespectful or insulting regarding anyone's current beliefs but rather to share information to assist in making an informed decision.*

Christian apologetics is the discipline that provides evidence and reasons to believe that Christianity is true. It has been practiced for centuries and is grounded in the Bible.[3] I have studied this topic for a number of years and earned a Master's degree in Christian apologetics from Biola University.

There are many great books on this topic, but my goal is to provide an easy-to-read story that shares some of this insight so that many who are unaware of this important information can be prepared.

If you are not a Christian, I hope this is helpful for you to consider the evidence in making your decision about committing to God.

If you are a Christian, I hope this book provides insight that will strengthen your love for God with your mind and perhaps increase your effectiveness in sharing your faith with others.

The following story is a fictional account about a family, but the evidence and rationale for God and Christianity that they discuss are real.

I hope the story is both entertaining and beneficial to your spiritual journey.

Let's begin.

PROLOGUE

Brazil—Present Day

The ten-year-old boy stood at the edge of the jungle. The sight of the ocean captivated him. Powerful waves crashed on the beach ten feet in front of him. The smell of saltwater filled his nostrils. The repetitive sound of rolling waves echoed along the beach.

The young boy had never seen anything like the vast ocean in front of him. He was accustomed to living in a dense jungle. To him, this new scenery was not only different but also interesting. Amazing. But part of the excitement was sneaking away to a location forbidden by his father. He had been told that this part of the jungle had too many dangerous predators.

The boy had no idea that an enormous snake slithered slowly toward him. The massive anaconda measured twenty feet in length and weighed over four hundred pounds. But it moved with stealth, making virtually no sound. Its scales slid slowly over the ground. The compression of dry leaves and crunch of small twigs were too faint to be heard. Its dark green color with large, black spots blended in perfectly with the surroundings. Its eyes, similar to brown marbles, had a sinister look. The snake fired its tongue in and out of its mouth. It had just emerged from a large swamp just a stone's throw away. The hungry snake was crafty as it slithered behind its unsuspecting target.

"Taaaaaaad!" the boy heard a voice say off in the distance—the kind of tone that was searching for someone.

The boy's eyes grew wide as he recognized his father's voice. His name was Tadeu,[4] but everyone called him Tad. He was struck with fear about getting caught and his potential punishment. He was not aware of the more immediate danger, being stalked by an enormous snake.

Tad considered two options—whether he should respond to his father or try to sneak back home. But inside he felt his guilt increasing, gnawing at his conscience. He didn't want to make things worse. He decided to take one last look at the view before answering his father. No doubt he would be reprimanded and not get a chance to come back here anytime soon. The sun glistened off the ocean water. The water line showed no end in sight. Tad wondered what huge sea creatures swam in such a massive body of water.

Suddenly Tad felt two spikes sink into the top of his back, next to his right shoulder. He immediately knew he was being bitten. Long, sharp fangs penetrated deep into the muscle between his neck and shoulder blade. A powerful jaw clamped on tight. The pain was intense. His knees buckled. The agonizing pain triggered a sharp, loud scream.

"Ahhhhhhhhhhh!"

Before Tad could raise his hands to try to pry the snake's head open, a coil of the snake had already wrapped around his torso. It squeezed Tad's arms to his body, locking them in place. The snake continued to wrap around Tad. He quickly lost control of his balance. Unable to stay upright, he fell to the ground.

Tad felt the snake tightening its grip. The constriction was slow but powerful. It was crushing. Tad was not able to fully inhale. He gasped for air. The pressure built, and Tad felt one of his ribs crack. The sensation of a bone breaking inside his body was terrifying.

At that moment, Tad felt extreme despair. Hopeless. He could not defend himself from attack. *There's no hope. I'm pinned and being crushed.* He lay on the ground waiting until the creature had finished squeezing the life out of his body.

I'm going to die, he thought to himself. *This is how I'm going to die.*

Suddenly Tad heard a smack next to his ear, shaking his whole body. A second smack followed. Tad realized something had struck the snake as it had stopped tightening. He still felt compressed, tightly locked, but the pressure was no longer building.

"Tad!" It was his dad's voice.

Several more smacks from his father's machete allowed him to unravel the snake's body from his son. His father grabbed Tad's face and looked into his eyes, apparently checking to make sure he was conscious and alive.

Tad's father then hugged him tight, fortunately not squeezing his broken rib. Tad felt his father quivering; his dad's body shook with emotion as tears of relief spilled onto his son's back.

Tad was lucky to have been saved, and it had a profound impact on his life. Many years later he would have the opportunity to return the favor by helping a US family that was visiting Brazil.

CHAPTER 1

Brazil—Twenty Years Later

"So where is God?" Lucy asked with a snide tone, clearly trying to start an argument. "Dad! Where is God?" The repeat of the question was louder and with a bit more disrespect.

Jack looked up from his book to see his sixteen-year-old daughter pointing at the television. Lucy had a scowl on her face. Her long red hair matched her fiery personality. She had always enjoyed arguing, about almost anything, and since they had started this church mission trip in Brazil at the beginning of the summer, religion was the current topic for debate.

"How can you sit there and read while the world is falling apart?" she continued with a snarl. Lucy had green eyes and a few freckles. She was a pretty girl, but the angry look on her face was much less attractive than her otherwise bright smile.

Jack restrained the impulse to snap back with a harsh reprimand, instead choosing to remain calm. Typically he would scold his daughter's disrespect and the situation would quickly escalate, leading to loud voices, sometimes slamming doors, and an eventual punishment. The cycle needed to change.

Jack shifted his attention to the TV, which had been on for background noise. The news showed the latest satellite images of Africa, which was now a place of devastation. The images brought back feelings of horror he experienced last week when a military task force from multiple nations bombed the entire continent in an attempt to eradicate D6—a horrific disease.

Although the bombings disgusted Jack, he recalled the fear that consumed the world. D6 was one of the scariest diseases in the history of humankind. Oddly enough, only humans contracted the disease; nothing in the animal kingdom. News reports had described the symptoms as beginning with a fever and muscle aches, similar to the flu, but they soon escalated to extreme fatigue and sharp muscle pain. After six days the disease was fully established and randomly attacked muscles in the body, stretching them beyond normal until they reached the point of tearing, rendering them useless. It was excruciating pain for the victim and became fatal when the random attacks eventually struck a vital organ, such as the heart. To make matters worse, the disease was highly contagious. Despite the best efforts from medical teams around the world, there was currently no vaccine or cure.

Jack ran his right hand through his black hair that was thinning and then rubbed the black-and-white stubble on his face, a day removed from shaving. He snapped out of the memories and refocused his blue eyes on the television. He winced at the video footage. Buildings that once stood tall were now piles of rubble. Cars were blackened from fire. And there were no people. Gone. Most had been vaporized in the bombings.

Jack felt an uncomfortable feeling of déjà vu. The horrific scene in Africa was similar to Australia. The painful memories he was trying to suppress flooded his mind. Just over two months ago, when Jack had first arrived in Brazil, the pandemic had reached emergency status in Australia, the place where D6 originated. Australia's borders were quickly closed and mass transit was shutdown, but despite their best efforts, they could not contain the spread of the disease across the continent. The transmission rate between people was very fast, and in just two weeks, it was virtually everywhere in Australia. It was difficult to know how many people were infected, but news reports at that time estimated the number of infected were as high as 80 percent of the population.

Initially Jack, and many others, did not fully appreciate the danger when it had first started on the other side of the world. But when the disease spread rapidly across Australia, panic escalated quickly. The global community feared other parts of the world would eventually be affected. That, in the opinion of government leaders, justified destroying Australia. Massive firebombs vaporized everything within the blast radius. Politicians from around the world gave speeches, attempting to justify the actions as a last resort to save humankind.

The global outcry against the bombings, killing millions of healthy people along with the sick, was widespread. But the sharpness of the protests was somewhat dulled by the fear everyone had of this disease. Deep down almost everyone worried this disease would literally destroy the entire human race.

Unfortunately, vaporizing Australia did not work. Various islands in the Pacific became infected, as some people from Australia had fled in small boats or planes to other landmasses. China, India, and Japan took extreme measures with their military forces to protect the borders of their countries. But some who fled eventually made their way to Africa, bringing the disease to a second major continent.

Regardless of quarantines facilitated by armed forces and medical personnel, the disease could not be contained. Just last week, the people of Africa suffered the same terrible fate as Australia.

However, because of the size of the continent, the amount of weaponry used on Africa was four times that of Australia, and it seemed to rock the entire planet to the core, causing movement in plate tectonics. Not only was the world facing a horrific disease, but plate movement was also beginning to cause sporadic earthquakes and volatile weather patterns. It really did seem as though the world was facing an apocalyptic crisis.

"Well?" Lucy asked sharply, while folding her arms. Her glare indicated she was still waiting for an answer. She started to tap her right foot.

Jack sat back, removed his reading glasses, and responded in a calm, loving tone, "Well … what do you think?" He sometimes responded with questions, trying to get his children to think for themselves.

Lucy seemed to take the bait. "Well if you don't have an answer, I guess I'll have to help you, Dad," she began with a verbal jab.

Lucy not only liked to win an argument but triumph with a confident and aggressive style. Jack knew Lucy had a good heart and was a truly kind and caring girl, along with being intense, passionate, and feisty. However, recent emotional pain from being too critical of herself in all aspects of life had influenced her approach to debating. Jack blamed himself for not observing her pain sooner. He felt guilt and an enormous burden to help her.

"I think if God existed, the world would look a lot different. He would stop diseases, earthquakes, dangerous storms, and so on. If this so-called God of yours is all-good and all-powerful, then He has the power and desire to stop that!" she stated with emphasis, again pointing to the television.

The proud look in Lucy's eyes indicated she thought she was pretty smart and had just made a point her father could not answer, leading to an easy victory.

Jack paused, waiting to see if his daughter would continue her tirade. She did.

"And on top of that, why did you have to bring us to this foreign country for an entire summer?" Lucy unfolded her arms, extended her hands palms up, and shrugged her shoulders. "Could you give that explanation another try? Because so far you haven't given me a good reason for ruining my summer!"

Jack wasn't surprised by Lucy's sarcastic gestures that accompanied her words. His daughter got quite animated when she was fired up for a debate. He was also not surprised by her second verbal attack. Most arguments this summer included her displeasure about this trip. It had been over two months now since they traveled from their home in the United States to Brazil for a summer-long church missions trip. Jack felt strongly that their two youngest children needed it. It took his wife, Sarah, some convincing, but eventually she agreed even though she was not able to join them.

The work focused on building and repairing homes for Brazilian families in a small village. They also handed out basic supplies as well as toys for children. Having fun with the kids seemed to be Lucy's favorite part; even though she didn't admit it to her father, she clearly enjoyed playing games with them. After a few hours of physical labor, soccer was the game of choice in the late afternoon. Jack and Lucy were amazed at how good the kids were at the sport.

Despite the outward complaining, the work to help the small Brazilian village seemed to be thawing Lucy's cold heart, just the kind of impact Jack had hoped for. But of course, there were times when Lucy clearly missed home and expressed her displeasure and desire to be back with her friends.

Jack felt a drop of sweat trickle down the side of his face. The Brazilian heat was uncomfortable. It had been two months and he was still not accustomed to it. A stand-up fan that swiveled back and forth moved the air around the room and provided a small amount of relief.

Jack reached to the side and grabbed a glass of ice water from a wobbly tray. He took a large sip of water and placed it back on the tray. The cold liquid was refreshing to his parched mouth.

Jack's eyes returned to Lucy. Her eyes were narrow with a sense of frustration. Apparently tired of waiting, Lucy broke the silence. She returned to her first point, attacking her dad's beliefs.

"Obviously you see the news. If your God existed, He would stop this horrible new disease that is spreading! Face it, Dad, God does not exist!"

The words were piercing to Jack's heart. He and his wife were Christians, along with their three oldest children, who were now in their twenties. But Lucy, child number four, was not following the family pattern of the first three. She was rebelling against most of her parents' guidance, including her religious upbringing.

The success of Lucy's older siblings seemed to play a part in her rebellion. Every so often she let out a comment to her dad that indicated she felt she didn't measure up to their success. Her father routinely reassured her that she was special and loved just the way she was. But Lucy eventually succumbed to her negativity about herself. Rather than attempt to follow in the footsteps of her siblings and risk the chance of falling short, she seemed to be rebelling, going astray, even if it brought grief to her parents. She resisted working hard at school, was hostile toward religion, and got in trouble in the neighborhood, purposely hanging around with the wrong crowd. It was that last concern that led to Jack's decision to make the missions trip last *all* summer, rather than just a week or two. Removing her from the wrong crowd was one way, although temporary, to protect her from bad influence.

But what Lucy didn't know was the degree to which her actions distressed her parents. It weighed heavily on them.

Jack had found success in various aspects of his life, including his career as a technology consultant. But he despaired over the direction Lucy was headed. All of the good things in his life seemed to get swallowed up by his concern for his youngest daughter. He blamed himself, constantly second-guessing previous decisions, as if they might have made the difference and changed her path. He and Sarah had spent hours discussing what was best for Lucy. One idea they had discussed was for her to see firsthand the reality of people living in different circumstances, being content with fewer material things. That was the catalyst for this long missions trip.

Peter, the youngest of the five children, was also a participant on the Brazil missions trip. He emerged from the third bedroom of the small, shabby house, scratching the top of his head. "Are you both arguing again?"

Peter gave a big stretch, indicating he had just gotten out of bed. He was fourteen, and although not as confrontational as his sister, he also expressed his displeasure to be spending the summer in Brazil. Unlike Lucy, who used sharp, biting words, he simply moaned about the current situation.

Peter was also different from Lucy in his approach to life. She was intense. He was a free spirit. He just wanted to enjoy the adventure of life and have fun. He seemed to be apathetic toward his parents' instruction about God. Jack sensed that Peter was going through the motions until he could leave home and truly make all his own decisions.

There was a pause in the discussion. Awkward silence. Stillness. Jack was troubled by Lucy's last statement. Her rejection of God had become more direct, and Jack was contemplating whether her barriers were emotional or intellectual. Maybe it was a little bit of both, but she certainly had intellectual questions he needed to help her with.

Peter looked at his dad and then his sister. His short, thick brown hair was a mess. His droopy eyes and slouched posture indicated he was still not fully awake.

Peter let out a yawn and then turned his back and headed for the kitchen. "I'd rather have breakfast than argue," he muttered.

Lucy ignored her brother. "Dad. Your silence indicates you don't have an answer. Why? Because there is no good answer. If God exists the world would not look like that!" For a third time, she pointed at the television.

Jack closed his book and put it on the table next to him. He shifted his position in his chair from relaxed to leaning forward, an indication he was going to respond. The old recliner creaked noticeably.

"Lucy," Jack said in a calm tone, "you say that if God exists, the world would not be filled with the horror we are seeing. But let's take a big step back and think about this." Jack paused to let her anticipation build a bit. Lucy opened her mouth, as if to interject, but Jack held up his hand, signaling he wasn't done. Lucy paused as

Jack continued. "If God does not exist, would Earth exist? Would the entire universe exist?"

"What are you talking about?" Lucy snapped. "Don't answer my question with your dumb philosophy."

Jack gritted his teeth behind his closed lips and decided to ignore the insult. Right now he preferred to make an important point, rather than reprimand. He took a small breath and continued. "Have you thought this through, Lucy? Let's see if you have. Did the universe have a beginning or has it existed forever?"

Lucy hesitated. She seemed to be pondering the question, perhaps wondering if she was falling into a trap. "Have you studied science, Dad? It's pretty obvious the universe had a beginning. Duh."

"Good. We agree that the universe had a beginning. Next point. Is it possible the universe popped into existence without any cause, or is it more likely that something, or someone, caused it to come into existence?"

A smirk emerged on Lucy's face, indicating she could tell where the conversation was headed. "Don't give me this philosophy baloney …"

Jack interrupted Lucy with a grin and pointed his finger at her. "You started this. You wanted to talk about God, which I'm glad to do. Are you going to answer my question or run from the conclusion? You're not a quitter, are you?" Jack said with a friendly smile.

Jack was playing to his daughter's competitive spirit. He continued. "If the universe had a beginning, does it need a cause? In other words, if there was a time when the universe did not exist, literally nothing, can the universe pop into existence by itself? Or does something have to cause it? Be honest."

Lucy shifted her stance and folded her arms. "Even if I say every effect needs a cause, that doesn't mean I agree that God was the cause. We have no idea what caused the universe."

"Good. So you agree that the universe had a beginning and it needs a cause. Stay with me. What are the main properties of the universe?" Jack asked.

"What?" Lucy looked disgusted. "I'm on summer break, not in a junior high science class."

"Yes. I realize you don't like to think too hard in the summer unless it suits your fancy." Jack was returning the sarcasm his daughter liked to employ. "I'll help you. The main properties of the universe are space, time, and matter. Right?" Jack asked, looking for agreement from his daughter.

Lucy's eyes widened, and her hands motioned upward, as if to say, *No kidding.*

Jack ignored her mocking gesture and continued. "Well, if the universe consists of time, space, and matter, doesn't it make sense that whatever caused the universe to come into existence is outside of time, space and matter?[5] In other words, the cause of the universe is timeless, spaceless, and immaterial."

Jack paused a moment to let Lucy get the point; then he continued. "Also, in order to create the universe from nothing, literally nothing, which means space and time itself had a beginning,[6] I would say that the cause is powerful.[7] Wouldn't you?" he asked with a level of gentleness, not the striking tone Lucy used.

Lucy seemed to be processing the point or trying to think of a counter.

Instead of waiting for a response, Jack decided to finish his overall point. "Finally, the cause is very likely personal. How is that, you may wonder? The act of creation indicates a decision was made. Whatever has always existed infinitely chose to make a change. A decision was made to create a finite universe. That something is either personal or impersonal.[8] But do impersonal things make decisions? Obviously not. Only personal agents make decisions. So it seems the cause of the universe is also personal."[9]

Jack saw Peter emerge from the kitchen, stuffing his face with a muffin. He was a typical teenage boy, eating anything he could get his hands on at all times of the day. He was tall for his age, having gone through a recent growth spurt the past six months. He was probably five foot seven, a couple inches shorter than Jack, who was of average size and build. Peter was rather lanky, as his weight had not yet caught up to his height. But standing next to Lucy, he looked even taller. She was clearly shorter at five foot three but a more athletic build than her thin brother, which stemmed from the running and swimming she did competitively.

Jack ignored the muffin crumbs falling from Peter's mouth. He returned his focus to Lucy. "Let's summarize and see what you think. The universe definitely had a beginning"—Jack paused a moment for emphasis—"and since it can't create itself, it needs a cause." Again, he paused. "That cause is timeless, spaceless, immaterial, powerful, and personal.[10] Does that sound like God?" Jack's tone was confident but gentle. Unlike Lucy, he was not interested in winning a fight. He wanted his daughter to really consider the point.

Jack noticed that Lucy had no expression on her face, other than perhaps her nostrils flaring a bit. They gazed at each other for literally five seconds without saying a word, as if the two had engaged in a staring contest. Peter interjected, breaking the silence, "Mmmm. Good muffin."

Jack broke off the staring contest to look at Peter. He was a bit more awake now and chewed on his food with a grin. Unlike Lucy, whom Jack knew was intense, Peter was laid-back and easygoing. He would rather have fun and joke about everything than engage in serious discussions.

Jack turned back to Lucy, who had not changed her expression. She seemed to be stewing inside, contemplating her next move. This was not the first time Lucy and Jack had discussions about God, but it was the first time Jack had offered this kind of response. In searching for a way to help his daughter, he began an intense study of Christian apologetics.[11]

Lucy finally countered. "Yeah, well, who created God?" she said snidely.

Jack furrowed his eyebrows. He was disappointed that Lucy seemed more interested in countering his point rather than considering it. He focused on subduing his frustration to take the edge off his response. "What do you mean, who created God? Only things that have a beginning need a cause. God, by definition, does not have a beginning."

"How convenient!" Lucy retorted. "You insert God to make your point and then you claim that the same question about beginnings doesn't apply to the almighty one." Her voice was escalating, as if being loud was a way to score debate points.

"No. You're misunderstanding the point," Jack said in a subdued, even-keeled tone. "Only things that have a beginning need a cause. God, by definition, is timeless. God is the uncaused cause. We already agreed the universe had a beginning, and based on the properties of the universe, we are reasoning that God is the best explanation. This is not conveniently inserting God; it's reasoning to the best explanation."

Jack stood up from his chair, which again creaked loudly, and continued to rock back and forth. "Look around at this house," he said, swinging his arms around for emphasis.

Jack and Lucy looked around the small, shabby house. It had one large space for the living room, which they were in. It was the central hub and provided access to the rest of the rooms: a narrow kitchen to the side, one tiny bathroom, and three small bedrooms. The walls were made with thin lumber. It had modest plumbing and electricity, some of which was visible between holes in the walls. The ceiling had patches of wood, which were obvious repairs. It was nothing like their beautiful, large house back home, but it served the purpose of providing them with shelter.

"Did this house pop into existence by itself?" Jack asked. "No. Someone made a decision to build it, and then people started the work to make it happen. Anything that has a beginning needs a cause, whether it's a house we live in or the universe we live in. But the creation of the universe is far more extraordinary; unlike a house, which is made from materials that already existed, the universe was created from nothing. *Consequently, one major reason to believe that God exists is the beginning of the universe!*"[12]

Lucy shook her head. "You literally have my head spinning."

"Let's make it real simple," Jack said. "Since the universe cannot create itself—someone outside of it caused it—God—"

Suddenly there was a loud knock at the front door. Jack immediately headed for it in case either Lucy or Peter might have thought about getting there first.

"Who is it?" Jack asked in a stern, deep voice.

"Tad. Can I come in?" His voice quivered with panic.

Jack recognized the voice and quickly opened the door.

"Thank you," said Tad, in between heavy breaths. He stepped into the house, one of several in the small village, and closed the door.

Tad's eyes, filled with fear, connected with Jack's eyes.

"D6 …" Tad panted. "D6 has somehow reached Brazil. So far it's one person that I am aware of. He is in a local village, not too far from here. No doubt the government is going to close the borders when they find out."

"Are you sure it's D6?" Jack asked. He was filled with panic, hoping Tad might be mistaken.

Tad paused to slow his breathing. "No question. Two muscles tears confirmed the diagnosis."

Jack didn't immediately respond, choosing to absorb the reality. He had promised Sarah to do everything possible to keep the kids safe. Although she was in agreement that the kids should go on this trip, she worried greatly about their safety. She had wanted them to come home when D6 ravaged Australia and the bombings took place, but the number of flights was greatly reduced, and ticket prices became exorbitant. They had also explored traveling by boat, but that also led to dead ends. After the disease hit and spread within Africa, getting home early had become impossible. They were just hoping that things would settle down to some degree over the next week and they could take their previously purchased flight home, which, so far, had yet to be cancelled. But now with this news about D6 hitting Brazil, they were in trouble. Big trouble.

Tad continued. "If you want to fly out, as we discussed, we need to leave ASAP."

Jack recalled their conversation. He and Tad had talked about the small plane Tad had acquired from his wealthy uncle. Tad had flown for many years. He had told Jack that he was indebted to him for all he had done, and when D6 invaded Africa and Jack could not leave Brazil early, they had discussed this scenario as a backup plan. They would flee Brazil to a small airport in the Caribbean and eventually make their way back home to the United States. Unfortunately the plane needed to be repaired with a couple new parts, which was only completed a couple days ago.

Jack was deep in thought. It was one thing to consider hypothetical situations, but this was now a reality. He wanted to get his kids home safely. Would leaving by plane be safer, particularly with the volatile weather patterns? But if they stayed, they risked the disease spreading to their location. And if the situation became bad enough, perhaps they too could face being vaporized by firebombs, similar to Australia and Africa.

Jack turned to Lucy and Peter. "We're leaving in fifteen minutes. Pack what you can."

CHAPTER 2

Jack noticed the hum of the aircraft engines. They had been flying for over an hour, but this was the first time there had been extended silence in the small airplane. The previous chatter from the four passengers had been a good distraction.

Besides the cockpit, there were eight seats in the plane, four on each side, with an aisle between them. Tad was in the cockpit flying the plane. Jack was in the cabin, first seat to left, with Lucy to his right and Peter behind him. Everyone was dressed comfortably—T-shirts, shorts, and sneakers.

Jack reflected on the brief phone call he'd had with Sarah before they took off. She was filled with panic. She agreed that it was best for them to leave, but she dreaded the worst and kept blaming herself for allowing them to go to Brazil in the first place, even though it clearly wasn't her fault. At one point, she was weeping hysterically, and Jack couldn't discern her words through her sobbing. He did his best to reassure her, but because they needed to hurry, they ended the call with her in tears. He was really looking forward to landing in the Caribbean to call her back.

Jack turned to his right to check on Lucy. She was looking away from him, out the window of the plane. He noticed the black clouds beyond her, to the right of the aircraft. Flashes of light exploded in the dark sky, signaling the danger of lightning. They were hoping to avoid a terrible storm that was headed for the coast of Brazil.

The plane bumped suddenly from turbulence. Jack saw Lucy

grab both armrests and look straight ahead. He knew that she hated to fly. Actually she was terrified. In a small plane like this, every jostle was sure to trigger a jolt of panic.

Even Jack was stressed. With each bump, he worried the turbulence might somehow damage the plane, causing it to lose control. There was no getting used to the fragile box of metal bouncing around thousands of feet in the air.

Jack looked again at the raging storm to the right. He felt a large knot in his stomach. A fresh coat of sweat emerged on his forehead, and he attempted to swallow the small amount of saliva he could muster. As nervous as he was, he worried about Lucy. She was motionless, stiff as a statue. He looked down at her hands and noticed her white knuckles, a sign of how hard she was clasping the armrests.

Suddenly Lucy snapped, breaking the silence. "Dad? You never answered my question! Why would a good God allow such dangerous weather!"

Jack thought about how to respond. *What would be a sensitive way to answer that question?* But then he wondered if Lucy really wanted an answer. Maybe it was a rhetorical question; perhaps she was just venting some anxiety.

The outburst was not uncommon for Lucy. Sometimes her fear turned to anger, causing her to lash out. The emotional pain she had inside from years of self-criticism had recently created a bit of a short fuse. She had always been an intense and passionate girl, and expected perfection from herself; however, more recently that intensity sometimes mixed with anger.

But even Lucy recognized that sometimes she went too far. One time she admitted to her dad that it bothered her a lot when she hurt people. She felt guilty but struggled to change her fiery approach. Jack had responded by hugging her and telling her he loved her. He comforted her and said that God made her special: a perfect combination of being strong-minded, along with a caring heart. But he also said it was important that she recognized there was a better way to treat people, as well as herself, and working to improve was a process. He also said that God loved her, and no matter what she did, God wanted a relationship with her.

Jack and Sarah even got Lucy some help, having her speak with church mentors and professional counselors. It helped a little, but Lucy still struggled with speaking her mind in a fiery manner. Before her grandfather passed away, he affectionately nicknamed her "Firecracker."

Maybe Lucy just wants to vent a little, Jack thought to himself. *A one-time outburst. I'm not sure she really wants to talk.*

He got his answer when she continued. "Look at the ugliness of that storm." Lucy again looked out the window. "If God exists, why would He allow that?" She took a deep breath. "Is He not capable of providing a better place for His human creatures to live?" Her sarcastic tone included a blend of anxiety and anger.

Several different answers ran through Jack's mind, including a couple of sarcastic responses against atheism. But he quickly dismissed them, as he was not the type to be disrespectful, and he knew that would not be helpful to his daughter, who was really distressed.

Jack exhaled slowly and shook the thoughts from his mind. Lucy was staring at the storm, perhaps checking to see if it was getting closer. He continued to wrestle with how to respond.

Then Lucy turned to look at her father. "Don't have an answer, do ya?" she said snidely. Her eyes were narrow. Her expression showed her annoyance and frustration.

What do I say? Jack wondered. He considered just providing some words of encouragement about the storm, but he knew his daughter better than that. It would seem hollow to her. He decided to use the opportunity to engage her in discussion; he would try to respond to her accusation against God, which hopefully would also provide a good distraction from the storm.

"I agree the natural world has problems. Everyone can see it is not an ideal place—"

"Obviously!" Lucy interrupted.

"But that is due to human beings having free will."

"What?" Lucy snarled, flashing a look of disdain.

Jack continued. "The recent earthquakes and storms are the result of man choosing to use destructive weapons, shaking the plates of the earth. That's not God's fault. Looking at the bigger picture, we live in a world that is affected by humankind's initial rebellion. God cursed the ground because of sin, the rebellion of Adam and Eve."

"Oh brother," Lucy said, rolling her eyes.

"Yes?" Peter jumped into the conversation with a sarcastic tone. "Oh sister, you called? I'm here."

"Shut up, Peter," Lucy retorted, flashing an annoyed scowl at what she clearly considered a dumb joke.

Jack ignored the sibling banter and decided to try to make a larger point. "Lucy, is it possible you are focusing on one small aspect of nature, where I admit there is chaos, and missing the extraordinary design in the world and universe that does allow us to live?"

Lucy rolled her eyes at her brother, as if to say he was not worth arguing with. She turned her attention back to her father. "Huh?" Her response didn't indicate that she didn't hear him; rather, it was a way of saying she didn't think his question made much sense.

"I really don't think there is much design, Dad."

Jack noticed her pausing, apparently waiting for a response. The dialogue seemed to be a good distraction for Lucy, as she had stopped checking the storm to her right. If it eventually caught up to them and started to shake the aircraft, there definitely would be no chatting. For now, the discussion was a good diversion.

Jack continued. "Look around at this plane we are in. Did it evolve from natural causes, like rain and wind beating on the earth over thousands of years, or did an intelligent person design and build it?"

"Dad, don't be stupid!"

Jack pointed at this daughter and said sternly, "Watch your words. I don't mind debating, but I won't tolerate outright disrespect."

Sometimes Lucy had trouble controlling her anger, and her responses included insults that wounded her adversaries. Jack tolerated a lot, but when she occasionally crossed the line, he felt compelled to discipline her disrespect.

"If you say something dumb, am I not allowed to call you out? Do you have an ego, Dad?" Lucy asked while raising her eyebrows.

Jack knew she actually had a lot of respect and love for her father. She had always been Daddy's little girl. When she was younger, she loved to do everything he was doing. Work around the house. Wash the cars. Throw the football in the backyard. But at some point she decided to rebel and go her own way. Sometimes she expressed remorse for her rebellion. For a few years now, she was clearly struggling with an emotional civil war—admiration and respect for father versus rebelling and following a different path. Her internal tug-of-war was obvious.

Jack continued. "Like I've said before, we both enjoy a good debate. You probably get that personality trait from me. But as your father, you will speak to me with a level of respect."

"Honestly, it's not you, Dad. It's your crazy religious ideas." Her eyes revealed her conflict. One time she had told her father that she really wanted to believe in God but couldn't; she was really struggling with intellectual questions. Jack got the sense that Lucy hoped he would convince her.

"Crazy?" Jack said. "I think God is a much better explanation for the world around us than atheism. That is *not hoping in spite of the evidence*; it is *believing and committing to follow God because it's the truth.*"

Jack scratched his forehead and looked around the plane. "Try to give this argument a chance. This plane is obviously designed and built by intelligent people. Even if we didn't already know that planes are built by people, we would reason that it is designed by an intelligent creator. What are the aspects of the plane that make this point obvious?"

Lucy sighed, somewhat annoyed at the question. "I don't know. It's obviously complex."

"Excellent!" Jack said, happy to get an answer without an insult. "There is extraordinary complexity. The plane is put together in a particular order for a specific purpose. Combining complexity and purpose equates to design and that requires intention.[13] Can intention come from random chance? Can intention come from nature?"

Jack paused, but Lucy didn't answer.

"No," he said. "Intention requires desire and intelligence."

"Dad, where are you going with this?"

"The plane is obviously designed by intelligent people because of the extraordinary complexity of putting together all the right parts in a way that allows the aircraft to fly. The universe and planet Earth also have extraordinary complexity with a purpose. They have just the right parameters that allow for the existence of life."

"Parameters for life?" Lucy retorted. "What are you talking about?"

Jack could see the flashes of lightning continue in the distance beyond Lucy. The storm looked violent. *Keep talking*, Jack thought.

"Gravity, for example. If the force of gravity did not exist and was not the precise force that it is, the universe would not allow for life to exist.[14] Another example is the strong nuclear force, which holds protons and neutrons together to form atoms. If it did not exist, and at an extremely precise value, the material elements necessary for life would not exist.[15] There are over a hundred parameters about the universe that are just right to allow for life to exist."[16]

Jack decided not to provide any more examples so as not to lose his daughter's attention.

"For the universe to support the existence of life, you need these parameters of physics to exist, and ..." Jack paused for emphasis.

"And each parameter has to be a very precise value.[17] That displays the intention of a divine architect."

"Are you making this up? How do you know all this?" Lucy asked skeptically.

"I've been studying Christian apologetics—evidence for Christianity."

"Evidence? You mean blind faith," she responded sarcastically. "No. Faith is not wishful thinking.[18] It is more like trust.[19] Faith is about believing something to be the truth, which can be based on evidence and reason, and deciding to put your trust in it. From my perspective, I believe it is the truth that God exists and that Jesus is the Son of God who was resurrected—all based on evidence. And I put my faith, my trust, in Him to save me from my sins that deserve punishment."

"Well, I don't see the evidence," Lucy said. "So there are a lot of complex aspects about the universe. I think random chance is just as good an explanation."

"Impossible," Jack said, shaking his head back and forth. "The mathematical probability of all of them existing and at just the right factors purely by random chance is mathematically impossible."[20]

"Wait a minute," Lucy snapped, clearly recalling an idea. "I read on the internet that there could be an infinite number of universes and our universe just happens to be the one that has the attributes to allow for life. Multiverse, I think they called it." She sat back and grinned. Jack could see the pride on her face, thinking she had just countered his point.

"The multiverse theory. Yeah, I've heard of it." Jack sighed. "Talk about unconvincing. Think about it. That theory suggests that there are an infinite number of universes that we cannot detect, with different attributes, such as different levels of the force of gravity, and we are here because our universe happens to have all the right attributes. The fact that we cannot detect these other universes does not sound like science. The whole idea sounds contrived to avoid God as the architect of our universe. If atheism has to go to this length to explain the design in the universe, I think that says something. And I think believing in God is far more rational."

"Blah, blah, blah," Lucy said, forcing a fake yawn. "Dad, you're beginning to bore me."

"I just made a pretty strong argument that the universe shows intention. Are you not the slightest bit impressed?"

Lucy answered as Jack expected. "Not really." She shook her head defiantly.

As Jack was looking at Lucy, he saw a giant flash of lightning explode in the sky in the window behind her. *Good thing she didn't see that*, he thought. Actually, he wished he hadn't seen it and hoped the storm wasn't catching up to them. He worried that Lucy would see him looking beyond her, out the window, so he decided to continue the conversation, keeping Lucy, and himself, distracted.

"Okay let's get a little closer to home. Consider Earth. You like to point out the negative things about Earth, but have you ever thought about all the amazing factors that allow us to live here?"

Lucy's face had no expression. She purposely blinked her eyelids slowly, as if to convey that she was not impressed.

"What if Earth was a little closer to the sun? What would happen?" Jack paused and extended an open hand, as if asking for an obvious answer.

"We would burn up," Peter responded.

"Hey, Dad's talking to me," Lucy said, flashing a scowl at her brother.

Jack couldn't see Peter directly but noticed his reflection in an opposing window. Peter tilted his head to the right, stuck out his tongue, and crossed his eyes.

Lucy's expression was that of annoyance with her younger brother.

"You're so immature," Lucy snapped.

Lucy was partially right. Peter was less mature than Lucy, but most of the time he acted that way on purpose to ignite her short fuse. However, there were recent events that showed that Peter was maturing. He was a great worker on the missions trip and participated in all aspects of the construction process without hesitation.

Jack considered Lucy's reaction to Peter and let out a slight grin. *Perfect*, he thought to himself. *Her competitiveness will keep her engaged.*

"Do you agree with Peter?" Jack asked.

"Fine. Yes. Earth would burn up if we were closer to the sun," Lucy admitted.

"What if we were farther from the sun?" Jack asked.

"Then I would move to another planet," Lucy joked. "I hate the cold."

"That's funny." Jack smiled. "But you get the point—Earth is at just the right distance to allow for life."

"Where are you going with this?"

"Stay with me." Jack extended his hand and nodded as if to reassure her that he was making a point. "Also, Earth rotates at just the right speed. If it were faster, wind speeds would wreck Earth. If the rotation were slower, then temperatures would prohibit life. We would burn up when we face the sun and freeze when on the other side."[21]

"So there a few interesting things about our planet that allow for life," Lucy quipped.

"Not a few," Jack answered. "There are hundreds of specific parameters required for a planet to allow for life to exist.[22] Earth and its respective, moon, stars, and galaxy have just the right parameters. Doesn't that seem to indicate a divine architect made this place for us to be able to live?"

"Yawn," Lucy stated, rather than actually doing it. "Are there not billions of planets in the universe? I'm sure there are many other planets with just the right factors, Father."

Jack thought he heard thunder and wondered if the storm was catching up. *Maybe it was just the engine*, he tried to convince himself. Apparently Lucy didn't hear it. The discussion continued to be the perfect distraction from the raging thunderstorm.

"There are a lot of planets.[23] I'll grant you that," Jack admitted. "But the chance of any one planet having all the necessary attributes is still extremely unlikely. One current estimate has the possibility at one chance in ten to the power of five hundred fifty-six.[24] That is one over ten with another five hundred fifty-five zeros. Those odds are so low we can't even really comprehend it. It means there are not enough planets to account for random chance. Our planet is perfectly designed to support life. Honestly, unless God designed another planet with these parameters, it is highly unlikely there is any other life in the entire universe."

"Wait. Aliens don't exist?" Peter chimed in with his dry sense of humor. "Sci-Fi movies are not true? My life is over."

Lucy turned to Peter and opened her mouth to say something but instead just rolled her eyes in disgust.

"I'm not convinced Dad," Lucy said, turning back to Jack and shaking her head. "What's your point?"

"My point is that the universe and Earth clearly show a design that could not have happened by chance." Jack paused for a moment and took a deep breath, wondering what else he could use as an illustration.

"Let's try one final design argument." Jack pulled out his cell phone.

"This is obviously designed. The physical structure. The hardware," Jack said as he tapped on the top of the phone, "and the software inside"—pointing to the apps on the screen—"are put together in a very specific, ordered manner that is required to enable it to function."

"When can I get a cell phone?" Lucy asked, attempting to change the direction of the conversation.

"When your mother approves. Good luck with that."

Jack continued. "Life on earth is extraordinarily complex. I marvel at our nervous system, circulatory system, digestive system, and so on."

"Are we going to argue about creation again?" Lucy asked.

Jack ignored the question. "How many cells are there in the human body?"

"A lot," Peter said.

Lucy glared at her brother. Again, Jack could see his reflection in the opposing window. Peter was grinning and nodding at his sister.

"That's right," Jack said. "The latest estimate I've heard is about thirty-seven trillion.[25] Whether it's actually more or less doesn't change the point. Either way, Peter is right—there's a lot."

"See, I'm smot," Peter said to his sister.

Jack smirked slightly. He knew Peter was bright, getting good grades in math and science. He frequently liked to play the sarcastic brother to annoy his sister, but Jack wondered if this time he was doing it because of his uneasiness about the storm. Unlike his sister, whose reaction to fear was anger, Peter tended to joke even more than usual as a way to cope with anxiety.

Lucy pointed at her brother and began to say something, but Jack interjected as her mouth was open. "Let's compare the cell phone versus one cell in your body. A cell versus a cell."

Lucy turned her attention back to her dad, her nostrils still flaring from her brother. "Huh?"

"Did you know that each cell in your body is far more physically complex than this cell phone?[26] All the various parts of a cell in the body operate in an orderly function. Is it more likely that this happened by chance or that there is a divine Creator?"

Lucy didn't respond, and Jack noticed that the flashes of lightning were definitely getting closer. Fortunately, with Lucy still turned to her left to look at her father, the dangerous flashes of light continued to go unnoticed from her perspective.

Again, he decided he needed to continue. "But not only is each cell in our bodies extremely complex physically, but there is also an extraordinary amount of information in each cell. Any guesses as to how much information in each cell?"

Lucy turned to her brother. "If you say, 'A lot,' I'll smack you."

"No. We treat our family with love and respect, right?" Jack interjected with a comment his children had heard frequently.

Lucy and Peter were actually quite close. Although they argued periodically, they had a bond that was closer than their other siblings, which was due to their closeness in age. She had always been a caring big sister to him. She helped him do little things when he was young: tied his sneakers, brushed his teeth, poured bowls of cereal for him. She comforted him when he was afraid of the dark. She protected him from bullies at school. She loved her little brother. Even now Jack knew she loved him. She had grown to be strong-minded and independent, and obviously a bit feisty, but Jack knew that deep down, she still had a tender heart for people, especially those in need.

"I'm sure you are going to say there is a lot of information in each cell," Lucy conceded.

"Yes. The DNA in your cell consists of two sets of three billion letters.[27] That is a lot of information. And DNA is important because it is the instruction manual to create the physical you.[28] That means your height, eye color, and so forth. DNA also tells your cells how to function, like healing a cut. DNA is similar to how the software, or code, in the apps of this phone tell the hardware how to function."

"Computer code," Peter muttered, as if contemplating the point.

"That's right, Peter," Jack said. "Actually Bill Gates, one of the founders of Microsoft, compared DNA to a computer program, but he said that DNA is far more advanced than software created by humankind."[29]

"What's the point, Dad?" Lucy snapped with a tone of exasperation. "You are stating a bunch of facts and then ascribing them to God. You really don't know this to be the case."

"You're right," Jack admitted. "We don't know. But we are trying to reason to the best explanation. To me it's obvious that DNA in the cells of our bodies is evidence of a divine Creator. It is not just millions of physical molecules. They are arranged in a certain way that contains information to help our bodies grow and function.

DNA contains a code with a purpose, and purpose has intention, which only comes from intelligence."[30]

Lucy didn't respond. Jack wasn't sure if her pause was because she was considering the points he was making with an open mind or thinking about a counterpoint.

"Information is immaterial. The message or purpose of DNA is separate from the material atoms,"[31] Jack said. "It is best explained by a divine mind—God."

Still no response. Lucy's face had little expression; it was as if she was really thinking about the point. She liked science, and perhaps she found this insight helpful.

Jack wondered if the intellectual barriers that Lucy held against believing in God were beginning to crack. He decided to summarize his points. "Characteristics of design are obvious throughout the universe. Design requires intention. Intention requires an intelligent being. *Consequently, another major reason to believe that God exists is design in the universe!*"[32]

Suddenly, Tad began shouting from the cockpit, "Jack! Jack! Come up here! Hurry!"

Jack unbuckled quickly and jumped out of his seat. He extended his arms against either side of the plane to protect himself from the possibility of being thrown around by unexpected turbulence. He quickly made his way to the cockpit.

Although it was nighttime, Jack could see clear skies ahead, which he knew was not the case to his right. The cockpit was filled with controls, switches, and lights, an intimidating sight to Jack, who knew nothing about flying a plane. "What is it?"

Tad turned to look at Jack. "A military jet. Behind us. It came up fast." His eyes were filled with panic. Tad had removed the headphone from his right ear but kept the other headphone on his left ear.

Before Jack could respond, a voice came through the headphones. It was loud enough that Jack could hear it faintly. "Unidentified aircraft. This is the US Navy. You are flying in a restricted zone and headed to a forbidden destination. You must turn back to your country of origin. Respond. Over."

Tad's expression grew even more nervous. "They want us to turn around and head back to Brazil."

Jack's eyes grew wide as he considered the thought of turning back. It was terrifying for multiple reasons, including flying into the teeth of the storm they were trying to outrun. "Tell him we are not going to the United States."

"US Navy, this is LJ316. We are not headed to the United States. We are going to a small island in the Caribbean. Over."

"Negative. You must turn back to Brazil. At this time no aircraft is allowed to leave South America. Over."

Tad became more desperate. "Please! You are risking the lives of the passengers on this plane if you force us to turn back and attempt to fly through the storm. Most people on board are American citizens. Over."

"Negative. You must return to your original departure. If you do not turn back, I will be forced to shoot you down. Over."

"Pilot! There are children on board. You must let us continue. Over."

"Negative. Your aircraft is being tracked by multiple sources, and I have orders. I am not able to comply with your request. Do not force me to engage your aircraft. You must turn around. Over."

Tad paused. He shook his head and looked up at Jack.

"I got the gist," Jack said to Tad. His eyes grew wide again as realized what must have occurred while they were attempting to flee. He muttered aloud, "News of D6 in Brazil must have gotten to the global leaders right after we left. They don't want anyone leaving."

Tad's expression turned from panic to dread.

"We're not gonna outrun a fighter jet," Jack said. "We have to turn around and take our chances in the storm. Tell him we'll comply. Hurry!"

Tad flipped a switch and spoke into the microphone. "US pilot, we will comply. I repeat—we will comply. We are turning now."

Tad flipped off the microphone and took a deep breath. He slowly started to guide the plane to the left to make a 180-degree turn. "Better head back to the cabin, Jack. Make sure everyone is buckled. It's about to get very choppy."

Jack didn't say a word. He turned and started to head back to the cabin. His movements were rather slow as his mind raced. He felt a deep knot in his stomach and goose pimples popping on his arms. Terror was overtaking his ability to reason—fear for his family.

Jack considered how he could hide his fear from his kids. Apparently he didn't hide his emotions very well as Lucy clearly noticed the worried look on her dad's face. "What is it? What's wrong?"

Peter asked, "Why are we turning around?"

Jack collapsed into his chair and grabbed his belts to buckle up again. "We are not allowed to proceed. The US Navy or global task force has closed down the airspace. We don't have a choice. We need to go back."

"What should we do?" Lucy asked with dread.

Jack turned to his daughter and replied without a hint of sarcasm, "Pray."

CHAPTER 3

Heavy rain was pounding the plane. The large raindrops hitting the roof sounded like bullets pelting the small aircraft. Lighting flashed all around them. The booming thunder was almost deafening; each one startling the passengers. But nothing was worse than the turbulence. It bounced the plane in all directions, as if hitting invisible speed bumps scattered throughout the air. After each bump, Jack tried to comfort Lucy and Peter.

"We're okay. We're okay." Jack had little fear for himself but did for his children.

They had been flying through the storm for fifteen minutes, about three-quarters of the way to get to clear skies. Lucy was barely conscious. She was clearly terrified and literally soaked with sweat. When they were first approaching the storm, she vomited every partially digested morsel sitting in her stomach, followed by several dry heaves. Jack, seated to her left, had held her arm throughout, trying to offer words of comfort. Her distress broke his heart.

Jack could tell that even Peter seemed shaken by the storm. He was unusually silent—no jokes or sarcastic banter. He didn't know what to do to help them. He just prayed and tried to offer some words of comfort.

"We're almost through it," Tad yelled from the cockpit. "Based on radar, another five minutes. Maybe less."

Jack felt some relief. He let out a small breath and looked

forward at Tad controlling the airplane. He felt appreciation and thankfulness that Tad was helping them.

When the two of them met a couple months ago in the village, Tad was in a dark place emotionally. He was deeply depressed at the death of his wife. She had just died about six months earlier attempting to give birth to their first child. The baby died too. Jack had learned from others in the village that Tad went through the stages of grief but was not coming out of it. He had started to make bad decisions as a way to cope with his emotional pain.

When Jack met Tad, he befriended him. At first, he simply provided support and friendship, but eventually, when it seemed to be the right time, Jack shared his Christian convictions. To Jack's surprise, Tad was already a Christian. Tad shared his story with Jack. He told him about a life-changing moment he had as a boy with a dangerous snake that had almost killed him. It made him really consider life after death. He said he had searched for the truth about heaven. He wanted hope, and he said he had found both truth and hope in Jesus.

But when Tad's wife and baby died, he fell into an emotional pit that he felt was too deep to climb out of. Jack spent considerable time with him, talking, praying, and doing a lot of listening. The love and support of a fellow believer was the medicine Tad needed to work through his pain. Although Tad told Jack he was indebted to him, Jack told him he didn't owe him; he was simply glad to help a fellow Christian. But now, in the airplane, he was appreciative that Tad was in a position to reciprocate and help his family.

Suddenly, a blinding light flashed through the windows, accompanied by exploding thunder, louder than ever. It literally rocked the plane. Panic erupted inside. Jack immediately thought that lightning had struck the aircraft.

"We're hit," Tad yelled, confirming Jack's initial thought.

Jack turned to Lucy. She was frozen, eyes wide and held an expression of terror. Jack grabbed her arm to console her, while asking his son, "Peter, are okay?"

"What happened?" Peter asked with panic.

"Lightning hit the plane." Jack answered as he looked around the plane, examining what might be damaged. Then he realized something was missing. The sound of the humming engine was no longer present. The sound of raindrops pelting the aircraft was even louder now.

"Tad!" Jack shouted.

"The engine is out!" Tad yelled back, clearly anticipating the question.

"Dad!" Lucy yelled. The terror in her voice was accompanied by tears.

"Stay here!" Jack ordered as he unsnapped his buckle and jumped out of his seat. He headed to the front, stumbling a bit as the plane was shaking from turbulence. As he arrived at the cockpit, he saw Tad feverishly flipping switches.

"I can't get it started," Tad said. "The electronics for the engine are fried."

All of the lights on the control panels and throughout the entire aircraft blinked off and then back on. They blinked again and then suddenly ... went out.

Darkness overtook the plane.

"Dad!" Screams came from Lucy and Peter in the back.

"Stay there!" Jack yelled back. "Stay seated!"

It was extremely eerie, floating thousands of feet in the air with no light.

Turning back to Tad, Jack asked with urgency, "What do we do?"

"We can probably glide for some time, but I don't think we can make it to the coast. We're still a ways out."

Jack could barely see Tad even though he was sitting right in front of him. The only light was the occasional flash of lightning. Dark clouds blocked light from the moon. Jack heard Tad flipping switches, but there were still no results.

Tad continued in a shaken voice. "Hopefully we will be past the storm and I can land the plane in the ocean. We need to get ready. Go to the back and open the closet to the left."

Jack turned to look at the back of the plane, which was pointless. It was pitch black.

"Dad?" Peter called out again.

"Wait, Peter!" Jack responded. His voice was not harsh but commanding.

"There are life preservers," Tad said. A large jolt of turbulence shook the plane, causing Tad to pause. Jack's hands that were braced against the walls stabilized him. He felt a heavy pit in his stomach and weakness in his knees. He was afraid for his children.

Tad worked to steady the plane and continued. "Also, get the large box at the bottom. It's the emergency raft."

Jack started for the back of the plane, his hands feeling around feverishly to make sure he stayed on track. Light was very faint in the cabin of the plane.

"What's happening?" Lucy cried.

"Dad!" Peter yelled again.

"Stay buckled!" Jack ordered, stumbling past them. His emotional side wanted to stop and console them. He wanted to explain the situation and reassure them as best he could. But his rational side knew he did not have time. They needed to prepare for the worst and quickly.

A few more steps and his hands connected with the back of the plane. Jack shifted to the left and frantically searched the smooth wall until his hand found the lever to the closet. He snapped it open and grabbed four life preservers.

Jack stumbled back through the plane and handed one to Peter and then Lucy. "Put these on."

Peter noticed first. "We're gonna crash!"

Lucy whimpered, "We're gonna die."

"Tad's gonna fly as long as possible," Jack responded. "But we might need to land in the ocean. We'll be okay."

Jack stumbled to the front and gave Tad a life preserver, placing it to the side. Jack could hear Tad still snapping various switches, but it was clearly futile. None of the switches triggered any response. Jack looked out the front of the plane, but it was very dark.

Tad spoke in a matter-of-fact tone. "No way to tell our altitude. We're definitely dropping though. We have some time, but you better get back there and buckle."

"Okay," was all Jack could mutter. The pit in his stomach got even heavier as he returned to the cabin. He took a breath, inhaling through his nose and exhaling through his mouth, trying to settle his nerves.

He checked Lucy and Peter. Peter had his life preserver on, but Jack needed to help Lucy, who was clearly shaken and fumbling with hers.

"I'll do it," he said as she continued to whimper.

He found the connections and snapped her preserver in place. He was about to collapse into his seat when he remembered the box with the raft. He staggered to the back of the plane and found the box. He quickly yanked it open and pulled out a giant, heavy ball of rubber. Jack staggered back toward the front, collapsed into his seat, and dropped the ball between Lucy and himself.

"What's that?" Lucy asked, her voice quivering.

"A rubber raft. We're gonna be okay."

There was no immediate response. But then Jack heard a small sniffle from Lucy. He grabbed her arm and repeated, "We're gonna be okay." He really didn't know that but felt compelled to reassure her.

Jack's hands fumbled to find his seat belt. It took a few moments, but when he located the pieces and clicked them together, he yanked it hard to ensure it was uncomfortably tight.

The plane started to have a little more light. It seemed as though the sun had just started to rise above the horizon and provide some level of visibility. There was no longer any turbulent winds or pelting rain.

Jack looked over to Lucy, who had returned to her frozen form, eyes closed, stiff as a statue. He was about to say something but noticed through the window that he could see the water in the distance. Some rays of sunlight were glistening off the water. Jack was thankful that they were still fairly high up.

"Tad? Are we past the storm?" Jack hollered to the front, looking to confirm what he suspected.

"Yeah, but slowly losing altitude. I still don't think we can make it to land."

Jack squeezed Lucy's arm to offer some comfort. "We'll be okay."

He closed his eyes to pray, something he had been doing a lot the past thirty minutes.

No one said a word. The lack of engine noise was unnerving—chilling. You could hear the wind outside gushing by. The plane was still fairly dark. It was both eerie and frightening.

Jack's prayer was fairly quick, and then his thoughts started to jump around. They moved from the current situation to his family at home. His wife. His heart ached for her, worrying how she would cope if something happened to them. His other children. He might never see them again. Things that seemed important days ago were so trivial and meaningless as they were facing potential death. Their mortality now seemed so fragile. He went back to praying. *Dear Lord, please be with us. I'm so afraid for Lucy and Peter and their souls. Please help us survive.*

Jack's eyes popped open, unsure of how long he had been praying and thinking. He looked out the window and could see they were getting very close to the ocean. It was sooner than he had expected. Before he could ask, Tad yelled to the back, "Get ready. We're close to impact."

Waiting for that first impact was terrifying. Jack could feel his heart pounding in his chest. He wondered if these were the last moments of his life on Earth.

The initial touch on the ocean rattled the plane, but Jack expected much worse.

The plane must have skipped off the water, he thought.

The second touch was much rougher. As Tad tried to settle

the plane down further, the impact worsened, shaking the plane violently. Screams filled the cabin for a moment, until they were overtaken by the sound of metal ripping apart. Jack's body jerked forward as the plane was stopping rapidly. His hands instinctively extended in front of him to protect his head, but his seat belt yanked hard at his waist, stopping the momentum.

It was a blur of chaos, but within seconds the aircraft had settled. Jack exhaled, not realizing he had stopped breathing. It was much brighter; light from dawn was coming in from some opening in the plane. But rather than look for the opening, Jack's first move was to check his kids. He could hear Peter unbuckling, but Lucy was not conscious. His eyes rapidly scanned her, but he didn't see any apparent injuries.

"Lucy!" he yelled, shaking her arm. She jumped into consciousness, eyes bulging, unable to speak.

"We crashed, but we're okay," Jack said. "Get out of your seat. Hurry!"

Jack scanned the surroundings as he unbuckled.

The plane had ripped apart into two main pieces. The cockpit was disconnected from the cabin; both pieces were about fifty feet apart, floating in the ocean, at least for the moment. The section that Jack and the teens were in had also split down the middle of the roof, showing the open sky above. Fortunately sunlight was emerging from the horizon, providing some visibility.

Jack grabbed the inflatable raft and ran to the front of the wreckage. Water had just started to seep into their section of the plane. Jack looked down at the darkness of the sea *Thank goodness we have a raft,* he thought to himself. He yanked a cord, and the giant rubber flotation device quickly sprang into form, filling with air.

Jack looked forward and saw the cockpit still buoying in the ocean. He didn't see Tad moving at all. He appeared to remain buckled in his seat.

Cupping his hands over his mouth, Jack yelled, "Taaaad!"

No response.

Jack yelled again, even louder, but again, Tad didn't move.

Jack turned to his kids, who had joined him. "Get in the raft before the plane sinks! Hurry!" The water seeping into the wreckage was accelerating quickly.

Jack jumped into the dark ocean. Most of his head submerged below the water for a moment until his life preserver popped him back above the surface. The water was warmer than he expected.

He began swimming to his friend, but each stroke was hard work. The life preserver was cumbersome, and his clothes were much heavier from being soaked.

The smell of saltwater was strong; splashes that got in Jack's mouth were a bitter saline flavor. He tried different swimming strokes to see what was easiest, but none of them were overly effective. He finally settled on a sidestroke that wasn't too strenuous.

But Jack was tiring quickly. The adrenaline he had been functioning on was fading. His breathing was heavy. He worried Tad might sink before he got there. He looked ahead and was relieved that the section was still floating. He lowered his head and continued swimming, laboring with weighty clothes. A wave splashed over his head, causing him to choke, but he fought on.

Eventually Jack reached his destination. Somehow the cockpit was still bobbing in the ocean; the nose of the plane was below the surface, facing down toward the deep. Jack grabbed a side of torn metal and carefully stepped onto the edge of the small cockpit, which was swaying at the mercy of the waves. At any moment it would fill with water and sink.

As Jack pulled himself into the wreckage, he called out, "Tad!" There was still no response.

Jack saw that Tad showed no signs of life. His left leg was bleeding from a metal fragment caused by the crash. A large contusion on his forehead indicated something had struck his head.

Jack shook Tad's right shoulder. "Tad? Wake up!"

Again, no response.

Jack checked for Tad's pulse but didn't feel anything. At that moment, Jack feared Tad had died from the crash, perhaps from a massive blow to his head. But he wasn't completely certain and couldn't just leave him in case he was wrong.

Thinking they only had seconds before the cockpit sank, Jack unsnapped Tad's buckle and tried to pull him from the seat. But Tad didn't budge. His left leg was wrapped in scraps of metal, holding him in place.

Suddenly water rushed into the cockpit, touching Jack's sneakers and then rising to his ankles. The buoying aircraft had succumbed to the waves. The water was rushing in fast.

"No!" Jack yelled, grabbing underneath Tad's armpits and yanking as hard as he could. But he was not able to move his friend. Water overtook him quickly, and within seconds, the entire cockpit sank. Jack took a quick breath just before submerging.

This first thing Jack noticed was the change in sound. Previous sounds of waves and his struggles were suddenly muted being underwater. The pressure of Jack's life preserver pulled upward, fighting against his descent as he held onto Tad. He pulled to no avail. He was sinking—rapidly.

He thought about letting go; but didn't want to give up.

Jack gave one final, desperate yank. The force of the cockpit sinking into the depths of the ocean aided in releasing Tad's body. But they were still descending.

Jack realized his life preserver was caught on some wreckage. His eyes bulged and his heart sank, thinking he was going to get dragged miles below the surface. He desperately smacked at the sharp metal that had snagged his preserver. A large bubble of air escaped Jack's mouth. He was losing oxygen quickly as he had not inhaled a full breath of oxygen before submerging.

Jack thought he might have to let go of Tad to try to unsnap his preserver. With one hand still holding Tad, Jack gave one final, frantic smack at the metal holding his life preserver and it released.

Jack held Tad tightly as the rest of the cockpit sank, disappearing into the darkness below. Still holding his breath, Jack looked up and saw the light of the surface above. He didn't know how far down he was. His lungs burned trying to hold on. He struggled not to breathe. He had no air left.

Any moment, he told himself. *Just hold on.*

With the help of his life preserver, they quickly rose to the surface. When they emerged, Jack gasped for air, taking deep breaths to fill his empty lungs. He choked on saltwater splashing from the waves. As he started to settle, he heard screams from Lucy and Peter, relieved he had surfaced.

"I'm okay," he yelled back to them. He choked out disgusting seawater, some of which he couldn't help from swallowing.

"Tad. I have you," Jack said aloud. He continued to hope his friend was alive, but he strongly suspected otherwise. Tad's body gave no signs of life.

Jack rested for a moment as the adrenaline that had helped him survive dwindled. As he continued to take deep breaths, he turned to look over his left shoulder to see how far away the raft was. *Maybe fifty feet.*

He mentally prepared himself for the swim and gathered his strength.

Holding Tad with his right arm, Jack began to swim backward. He kicked with his feet and swished his left hand underwater, slowly pulling them toward the raft. The labor was difficult and progress slow. Kicking his feet while wearing sneakers was particularly challenging.

The hardest part was fighting against the powerful waves. Most of waves caused them to rise, halting progress until they leveled out again. Occasionally water splashed over Jack's head, causing him to spit out the salty liquid. There were still no indications of life from Tad.

Jack paused for a moment to take a break. He was exhausted. He had been swimming for about five minutes and was not quite halfway to the raft. Lucy and Peter had been encouraging him and giving progress updates as he closed the gap. Jack took a deep breath and continued.

Only about twenty-five feet left, he thought.

Suddenly, the voices of his kids changed from encouraging to panic.

"Daaad!" Peter screamed in a way Jack had never heard him before. "Sharrrrrrrk!"

Jack saw Peter pointing ahead, back where the cockpit had submerged. A large, dark gray fin protruded out of the water. It was sideways, not facing Jack—yet.

Jack felt a rush of panic. He was completely vulnerable in the water, still a good distance from the raft. He wondered what he would do if the shark started to swim toward him.

As he kept swimming, he recalled the image of Tad's bleeding leg when he was still in the cockpit. By now they had been in the water for about ten minutes, so who knows how much blood had leaked into the ocean. It suddenly occurred to Jack that there might be a trail of blood leading straight to the two of them.

Jack closed his eyes and kicked feverishly. Lucy and Peter pleaded with him to hurry. Jack's muscles were fatigued; it was his adrenaline that enabled him to continue.

Lucy screamed in horror, "Daaaaad!"

Jack didn't even look at Lucy. He knew what that meant. He looked forward and saw the large shark fin pointing in his direction. He noticed how large it was, and then suddenly, it descended below the surface.

"Tad. I have you," Jack said. They were still about twenty feet from the raft. He tried to kick, but his sneakers made it difficult. His clothes were heavy. It was like swimming in a murky swamp.

Suddenly, Jack felt Tad's body ripped from his arms, yanked below the surface. It was almost instantaneous. There was no time to react. Tad was just gone.

Jack reached below the water in front of him, swishing urgently, but his friend was nowhere. Jack paused for a moment before he fully realized what had happened and the potential danger to himself. Some behemoth sea creature had just easily snatched his friend from his arms. And it might prey on him next.

Jack turned toward the raft and frantically swam for safety. Every ounce of adrenaline aided his movement. His lungs burned. He choked on water, splashing all about. Lucy and Peter screamed for him to swim faster. With each stroke he wondered if something might be approaching from below, ready to open its mouth and bite his legs. If something did grab him, how could he break free? At this point, maybe there were multiple sharks. He felt extremely vulnerable in the vast ocean, not knowing if something was pursuing him.

Jack sensed he wasn't able to swim fast enough. He paused to unbuckle the life preserver. Stopping might be foolish, but he simply needed to swim faster. He unclicked the preserver and began to yank it off. He had a terrible feeling, as though at any moment he would feel a bite from sharp teeth. Maybe a large mouth would swallow both legs at once. Maybe he would get dragged underwater.

He wondered for a moment if he should go below the surface to see if anything was approaching but decided that would just waste time. He resumed his frantic freestyle strokes, cutting through the water as fast as possible. He splashed feverishly. Lucy screamed at a high pitch just as Jack reached the raft.

Jack hurled himself upward onto the raft, getting his arms and part of his torso into safety, but his feet still hung in the ocean. Lucy and Peter yanked at his body, edging it farther into the raft, but Jack's feet dangled in the water. Jack kicked hard, pulling up with his hamstrings to get his feet out of the water. He made it into the raft, and the three of them rolled away from the edge.

They each lay motionless in the raft next to each other. No one said a word. The only sound was Jack's heavy breathing and the waves slapping against the raft.

Feeling secure, at least for the moment, Jack placed his right hand over his eyes. He fought back tears. His emotions were overwhelming, almost uncontrollable. The reality of crashing and then losing his friend in a horrific manner were beyond words. Jack was mentally tough. It was unusual for him to get emotional, but hours of panic and now deep sadness had pierced his strong disposition. He had feared losing his children in the crash and had now actually lost his friend.

The only reason Jack didn't release an avalanche of emotions was that he knew he had to be strong for his teenage kids—physically and emotionally. He lowered his hand, sat up, and examined the situation. Other than some floating debris, the entire plane was gone, two separate pieces sinking deep toward the ocean floor.

He took his cell phone out of his pocket, dreading the worst. It was clearly dead. It had already run out of battery life long before, but now the ocean water had gotten inside. Bubbles showed inside the screen.

Jack looked around and saw that there was no land in sight in any direction. He hoped that maybe someone had seen the plane crash and might come to their aid soon.

But what if no one was around? He wondered how they would survive. Fortunately there was no heavy rain or waves right now, and the sun was ascending. The circle of light was on the edge of the horizon. Its rays were getting stronger, and Jack needed the heat to dry his clothes and warm his body.

He appreciated the light from the sun. It was such a stark change from being in the darkness of the plane for so long. Then a scary thought occurred to Jack. Obviously at some point, the sun would be on the opposite side, descending out of sight, leaving them again in darkness. Even with some light from the moon and stars, it was an eerie thought to be in a rubber raft, bobbing in the vast ocean, surrounded by darkness.

CHAPTER 4

It had been five days of drifting. There was no land in sight. The first couple of days had been filled with fear: fear of the massive, powerful ocean around them; fear of predators lurking below; and fear of never being rescued.

The nights were the worst. The sounds of the ocean, shrouded in darkness, were downright chilling. Sea creatures periodically surfaced, seemingly close to the raft. One time the moaning of a huge whale was too close for comfort. Occasionally large waves slapped against the rubber raft, shredding the nerves of its passengers. They worried the raft might flip, removing them from their only security, making them vulnerable to predators.

But over the last couple of days, despair had begun to surpass fear. Hunger and thirst were mounting. Fortunately the weather had been helpful. An occasional light rain had provided an opportunity to get drinking water. Although their attempts at fishing had failed, Jack had scavenged a bunch of packaged food from the plane debris that had been floating on the surface, taking the risk of jumping into the ocean to retrieve them, despite the pleas of his kids.

Nonetheless, their food intake was not nearly enough. Their bodies craved more calories and had resorted to consuming body fat. Jack felt it was necessary to ration the packaged food they had, eating just enough to stay alive. The granola bars, chips, and candy were tempting in their state of hunger, but they needed to be smart about using this limited food supply. Surprisingly, Lucy and Peter were in agreement with rationing the food.

Jack had attempted to maintain the spirit of his kids while also doing the same for himself. They had reminisced about good memories—family vacations, nights of playing board games, going to the movies, and other fun times. They each shared their favorite moments. Peter liked the times when they would laugh together about the quirky things that made their family unique. Lucy recalled a vacation memory with the entire family. She was a small child and the entire family had gone to an amusement park. Surprising to Jack, she even admitted that she regretted recently withdrawing from family events; she would give anything to be back in those moments. For Jack, the best times were not about himself but seeing his family have fun. But eventually all the memories faded away and they were pulled back to reality.

Jack stayed optimistic on the outside, but inside, his emotions were at war. His positive demeanor and strong faith in God faced constant attacks of despair as he feared the reality of their situation. There was no hope in sight. No land. No boats. No planes. Just drifting in the sea, which seemed to go on forever in all directions. The sun was taking its toll on them as well, burning their skin and draining fluids from their bodies.

Jack worried about his wife; he wondered how she was coping with the unknown. Sarah had been frantic before they departed Brazil in the small airplane. Now that he hadn't called in a number of days, she would certainly have assumed the worst. Jack reminded himself he needed to be an emotional rock for Lucy and Peter.

They were each sitting against the edges of the raft, something Lucy would not have done the first couple of days for fear of sharks. No one was saying a word. There was not much left to say or do, except sit and wait, avoiding the use of unnecessary energy, hoping to be found.

It was the middle of the day. The sun was directly above, beating down rays of oppressive heat. Jack felt his dry tongue touch the roof of his parched mouth. He grabbed one of the water bottles they had used to capture rainwater and took a small sip. Swooshing the liquid around his mouth brought indescribable relief. He closed his eyes to enjoy the moment. He felt he could fall back asleep but heard movement in the rubber raft. He realized just how lethargic he was when he needed to gather energy to force his eyes open. Through half-opened slits, his eyes saw Peter extending an open hand, indicating his desire for water as well.

Jack began to lean forward to give him the bottle but paused when he heard a faint sound off in the distance.

"What?" Peter asked.

Jack lifted his left index finger to his lips, signaling a request for quiet. His adrenaline kicked in, providing a jolt of energy. He sat up onto his knees.

Lucy's head swiveled back and forth, as if looking for potential danger, not sure what her dad was doing. Then she faced the same direction, apparently trying to detect what he was hearing.

Jack heard the faint humming of a boat engine. He dumped the contents of his survival bag next to him. The collection of items included a folded pocketknife, two small flashlights, a compact pair of binoculars, some waterproof matches, fishing line, two small books, and a flare gun. Some of the items were retrieved from the plane's debris and some came with the emergency raft.

The flare gun was what he wanted. He quickly picked it up and raised his arm. He closed his eyes and prayed that the gun would work. He worried that water had somehow rendered it ineffective.

Jack squeezed the trigger. He was relieved to hear the pop of the gun, firing the contents high into the sky. The red flare was bright, even in the middle of the day.

The three desperate family members all looked toward what appeared to be a small fishing boat.

Please God, Jack thought to himself.

After a few seconds, the boat seemed to alter its course and begin moving toward them. The hum of the engine was getting louder. Jack waved his arms frantically in the air. Lucy and Peter followed his lead.

Jack felt tremendous relief sweep away all of his negative emotions, overtaking his fatigue, hunger, and despair.

Peter stammered in a faint voice, "We're … we're saved." Tears began to trickle down Lucy's face. The emotions of being rescued from hopelessness were overwhelming.

The fishing boat closed the distance in no time. It was about twenty feet in length. The saltwater had taken a toll on the white paint. There were several scratches and divots in the wood, a sign of decades of action. It was old and worn but clearly operational.

Jack noticed a large, round-shaped man controlling the wheel. He looked to be a bit older than Jack, probably in his midfifties. His faced was filled with facial hair—a black and silver mustache and beard. He wore an old skipper's hat that was stained from years of sweat. He was the only passenger in sight.

Jack heard a few thunderous barks from what sounded like a large dog, but he didn't see the pooch.

The boat pulled up along the raft. Jack flashed a smile at the skipper. "We're so glad to see you. We thought we'd never be found."

The skipper didn't respond. He was searching for something inside of his boat. He finally bent down and pulled out a large rope. He gathered some excess and tossed the rope over to Jack, who caught it in mid-air

"Tie this to somethin' secure," the skipper said in a deep, raspy voice.

Jack found a large rubber loop in the raft and began to knot the end. He felt such relief. He had to control his emotions so he wouldn't lose his composure. It was amazing how quickly their situation could change. Just moments ago he had felt despair, but almost instantly, his feelings had changed to hope. His body felt energized. But just as he finished double knotting, he heard the panic of Peter's voice. "Dad!"

Jack looked up and saw an expression of shock on Peter's face, staring toward the boat. Jack turned to see the skipper pointing a handgun at them.

"What are you doing?" Jack pleaded.

"Survivin'," the skipper grunted through his yellow teeth.

Jack paused, dreading the worst. He lifted his hands slowly, signaling his submission to the threat. "What do you want?"

Before the answer came, Jack started considering his options. The skipper was way too high and far to lunge at. There was nowhere to hide in the raft, which was now securely fastened to the boat. If the situation called for it, the only escape might be for he and his kids to jump into the ocean, leaving the raft behind.

"I don't need yur tools," the skipper grunted. "Got nuff junk of my own," he said, looking around at the contents of his own boat. "But I'll take that pile of tasty food," he said, waving the barrel of the gun in the direction of the wrappers of granola bars, chips, and candy. "Yeah. That looks tasty."

Jack paused, somewhat relieved that was all he wanted but concerned about giving away their last bit of food. But there really was no decision.

"Okay," Jack said.

"Dad!" Peter barked, apparently dreading the thought of no more food.

"We have no choice," Jack responded, gathering up the food and squeezing it into the bag that previously held the survival items.

Jack turned to the boat and paused. "Cut the rope and I'll throw you the bag."

"Yur not in position to give orders," the skipper grunted. He raised the gun a little higher, as if to remind Jack of the threat.

Jack extended his arm over the raft, in a manner that threatened to drop the bag into the ocean. With the weight of its metal buckles, it would probably sink. Jack was betting his life that the hunger of the skipper would be enough to give in to the demand. He wondered if this ultimatum was wise, but for some reason, he feared that if he simply gave the food, the skipper would make another demand. Although there was no way for them to flee, he felt that having the raft tied to the boat made them more vulnerable.

Jack watched the hammer of the gun intently; if it moved even slightly, he had decided he was going to run to his kids and push them into the ocean, while jumping in himself.

But there was no reaction from anyone. No one moved or spoke. It was a standoff. Everyone was waiting to see if the other person would move first.

Jack felt a drop of sweat run down his cheek. Despite the swaying of the raft, he remained steady. Focused. He showed no sign of wavering from his demand.

The skipper finally broke the stalemate. "If you don't throw the bag when I cut the rope, I'll shoot. Believe me. Whether I hit you or yur raft, y'all be done for."

Jack nodded, agreeing to the terms.

The skipper lowered the gun in his right hand and slowly lifted a machete with his left hand. He slammed the machete against the side of his boat, slicing the rope with one hack.

Jack saw the tension of the rope collapse, confirming the rope was severed. He didn't hesitate in meeting his end of the bargain. He immediately threw the bag to the fishing boat.

The skipper caught the bag in midair with his left hand, which apparently had dropped the machete. He lowered the bag with his left hand and slowly raised the gun in his other hand toward the raft.

Jack felt a massive pit in his stomach. His eyes bulged in terror. The raft had barely started to drift away; it was still very close. Jack was just about to order Lucy and Peter to jump out of the raft, but then the skipper laughed loudly and dropped the gun inside his boat. He grinned and buried a hand in the bag. A sinister smile emerged as he removed a candy bar. He tore it open and took a big bite. A large German shepherd appeared, placing his paws on the side of the boat and extending its snout, begging for food. The skipper glared at Jack, gave a slight chuckle, and handed the remainder of the candy bar to his canine companion.

"Good luck to ya," the skipper said sarcastically, followed by a loud, wicked laugh. He turned away and slammed the engine into gear, driving away from the raft.

As the boat proceeded away from them, Jack felt relief. The immediate danger was gone. He recognized they no longer had food, but things could have been worse. They could have been left without the security of the raft or been taken prisoner or shot. He didn't want to dwell on other terrible possibilities. He needed to gather his thoughts and think about what was next.

The three of them plopped themselves down in the raft. No one said a word. The mood was clearly somber. As quickly as hope had risen, it was gone, like filling a balloon with air and then puncturing it with a pin. It was gone in an instant. No more hope. Back to despair.

Jack grabbed a small backpack he had scavenged from the plane debris. He gathered the survival items that had been in the other bag and placed them inside. Jack decided to break the silence with words of reassurance. "We're gonna be okay." His eyes met Lucy. She had a scowl on her face. Jack looked to Peter, but his head was down, as if in deep thought.

Jack repeated, "We're gonna be okay. We can't see land yet, but we are definitely drifting in that direction. Rain will come and provide us with enough water. We need to trust God."

Jack had barely finished his words when Lucy snapped, "Trust God?" Her tone was that of annoyance and disgust. "What just happened is one reason I don't believe in God."

"Why do you say that?" Jack asked in a calm, genuinely caring voice.

"Isn't it obvious? If God existed, wouldn't He be trying take care of us?" She made air quotes for the word *trying*, as if to indicate that God was not capable. "I know you, Dad. I'm sure you've been praying for days on this raft. And God responds by sending someone to threaten us and take our food? Give me a break." She folded her arms and looked off in the distance. She was clearly filled with anger, more than worry or sadness.

Lucy took a drink of water as Jack wondered if responding was appropriate. Maybe talking would take their mind off things and help the time to pass. This might be an opportunity to speak about spiritual hope.

While Jack was wrestling with his thoughts, Lucy broke the momentary silence. "No response, Dad?" she asked. Lucy paused only a moment before continuing. "Evil. You can't reconcile it with God's existence. You can talk all you want about creation and the design of the universe. But what just happened is one reason I don't believe that God exists."

"Actually, what just happened is one reason I *do* believe that God exists," Jack countered.

"What?" Lucy snapped. "I think the heat and lack of water are getting to you, Dad."

Lucy sat up straight and focused her attention on her father. It was as if she had received a jolt of energy and was hoping for an argument. "That's ludicrous, Dad, even for you. You're telling me that if God exists, He wouldn't have stopped that guy from stealing?" Her voice began to escalate. "If God is all good and all powerful, wouldn't we still have our food!" she exclaimed, waving her hands at the now-empty spot on the raft.

"Do you think morality exists, Lucy?" Jack asked. "That there are good and evil actions?"

Not waiting for her to respond, Jack continued. "Of course you do. We just experienced an evil act. Every rational person knows that there is a standard for right and wrong behavior. But where does this standard come from? What is the source of morality?"

"Oh brother," Lucy retorted, rolling her eyes.

She then quickly pointed at Peter, a threatening sign that she didn't want a dumb comment from him. Peter looked surprised at her gesture. Then a smile emerged as he realized what she meant. He snapped his fingers, indicating disappointment that he had missed the opportunity to antagonize his sister.

Lucy turned back to her father. "I suppose you're going to suggest that the Bible is our source for morality."

"I didn't mention the Bible yet. I asked you what the source of morality is."

Lucy extended her arms. "People. Societies. The world. We don't get morality from an ancient belief about a bearded man floating in the sky. We get it from people."

Jack ignored the insult to stay on point. "So if I can show that morality cannot be from humankind, but rather requires an independent source, a source beyond people, isn't God a reasonable explanation?"

"Tall task, Dad," Lucy quipped. "Tall task."

Jack thought to himself, *This may be a lengthy discussion or Lucy may tune me out quickly.* He took a drink of water and shifted his body to get a little more comfortable in the raft. He then asked, "What did the skipper do wrong?"

Lucy rolled her eyes. "Stole our food. Duh," Lucy chirped, clearly annoyed at the need to provide an obvious answer.

"Is stealing wrong only because of the way you feel inside? Or is the action itself wrong?"[33] Jack asked.

Lucy crumpled her eyebrows and frowned, indicating she didn't really get his point.

Jack continued. "I think it's pretty obvious that the action of stealing is wrong. It is not wrong simply because of our feelings," Jack said as he touched his chest. "Even if we feel it was wrong and maybe later the skipper has guilt about it, the reason stealing is wrong is because the action itself is wrong, not just because of the way it makes us feel.[34] In fact, if someone stole something from you, but you were not aware of it, the action would still be wrong."

A wave came by and lifted the raft slightly. It reminded Jack of his surroundings, but it didn't seem to distract Lucy.

"What's the point?" Lucy asked with a tone of impatience.

"That morality is not based on your subjective feelings. Certain actions, regardless of emotions, are right or wrong. This makes morality objective, separate from people."

Lucy fired back, "No! Society has made rules so we can all

coexist and thrive. Stealing is wrong because it hurts others, and we could never survive if that was acceptable. People have been conditioned by this fact. Society has made the rules!"

"What society?" Jack waved his hands around the ocean. "There is no society or country out here. Yet stealing is still wrong, isn't it?"

Jack looked at Peter and then back at Lucy. He leaned forward to ensure he had both their attention. "I want you both to get this. Morality doesn't come from people. Here's why. If parents, like the skipper, taught their children to steal, would that make it right?" Jack looked at both of them. "Obviously no. If an entire country decided it was okay to steal resources from another country simply for selfish desire, would that make it okay? Again, clearly no. Why?"

Jack paused to wipe away a coat of sweat that had formed on his forehead and then continued. "This is because the standard of right and wrong exists beyond humankind. Our opinions don't change it. If someone says that stealing or slavery are good, we don't say, 'That's good for you but not for me.' We say they are wrong!"

The facial expressions of Lucy and Peter were almost identical. They looked puzzled. Either they were trying to understand Jack's point or thinking of a response. Perhaps both.

Jack finished the point. "God is the best explanation for morality. Why? Because to have moral rules that are objective, true regardless of people's opinions, yet also applicable to all humankind, it must have a source that transcends humankind."[35]

"Then why do some countries have different rules for morality, oh smart one?" Lucy challenged.

"They generally don't," Jack answered. "For the most part, societies have very similar rules about morality.[36] Murder is wrong, theft is wrong, and so on. The differences tend to be around the edges, or they may have radical, false ideas to justify bad behavior."

"I'm not buying it," Lucy stated.

Jack lifted each of his calves, which were beginning to stick to the hot raft. From the end of his shorts to the edge of his socks, his legs were red. They had been sunburnt for some time, but now he noticed bubbles beginning to form, indicating the burn was escalating from first-degree to second-degree. He folded his legs inside to hide them from the scorching sun. Pressing his red shins against the raft stung, but it was better than risking further damage. Lucy and Peter were also burnt but less so. Jack had used some clothes and debris from the wreckage to shield their skin as much as possible.

"Do you have a favorite type of music?" Jack asked, already knowing the answer.

"Of course," she stated, folding her arms, as if again clearly annoyed at having to answer an obvious question.

"Is the music you like different from your brother?"

Lucy sighed.

Jack knew the answer was an obvious "yes" but wanted her to say it to follow the point.

"Of course," she admitted.

"Is your music right and his music wrong?" Jack asked.

"Try the other way around," Peter quipped. "My music is clearly better."

"No. It's personal preference," Lucy countered.

"That's right," Jack agreed, pointing at Lucy, as if that was the answer he wanted. "The truth about which music is best is subjective. The topic of favorite music is based on personal preference. It comes from inside each person."

"Where are you going with this?" Lucy snapped.

"Is morality the same thing?" Jack asked. He could see by the look on both their faces they were still trying to get it. "Is morality based on personal preference, like favorite music? We think stealing is wrong, but the skipper thought it was good. He justified the action, so does that make it okay?"

"No. It's wrong, even if he thinks it's okay," Peter concluded.

"Exactly!" Jack stated emphatically. "Morality is not subjective. It is objective. The truth of morality exists separate from our opinions. But if that is the case, then morality is not grounded in humankind. The source of this moral standard must be beyond humankind.

What is the best explanation of this source? Where does morality come from?" Jack paused and then concluded, "God provides the standard of goodness."

There was silence for several seconds, as if everyone was reflecting on the point. Jack couldn't tell what they were thinking. Maybe the heat was slowing everything down, including their ability to think clearly.

Lucy smiled, as if the perfect response had suddenly occurred to her. "All right, Dad. You think you're so smart? Now you can answer one of my questions. Is something good because God says it is good arbitrarily, or does God tell us to act a certain way because goodness exists separate from God?"

Jack nodded, understanding the point Lucy was trying to make. "This is called Euthyphro's dilemma."

"Eutty who?" Peter asked.

"A little background, Peter. Plato was a Greek philosopher who lived many centuries ago. He tried to make the point that morality cannot be explained by God. He reasoned that there are only two options regarding God and morality, and they are both a problem. Either God can change moral rules arbitrarily, to be whatever God so chooses. In other words, God could have decided that stealing could be good or bad."

Jack shook his head. "But this option doesn't work. It clearly seems contrary to our moral intuition. It does not seem to make sense that God can change goodness."

Jack held up two fingers. "Option two? Morality exists separate from God. In other words, God is not the source of morality; He simply tells us about rightness or wrongness, which exists separate from Him. But this is also a problem since it would mean that God is not sovereign, ruler of all. Since neither of these options seem acceptable to Christians, then God must not exist, goes the argument."

"Well, what's the answer?" Peter asked, clearly intrigued.

"The bottom line is that this is a false dilemma that was solved a long time ago. These two options are *not the only options*. There is a third option that actually makes sense—the standard of goodness is grounded in God's nature.[37] God's moral commands come from His goodness. They are not arbitrary or changeable. Nor do they exist separate from God. They exist out of God's character."

"This is deep." Peter said. "I don't know that I have the brain power to process this right now," he said in a sarcastic tone, raising his hand to his forehead.

"You don't have the brain power, period," Lucy said, taking the easy opportunity to lob an insult. Turning her attention back to her father, she continued. "You're making this more difficult than it needs to be. The bottom line is that I don't need God to tell me what is right and wrong. I simply know it."

"Exactly," Jack said, pointing at his daughter. "God has wired it into your conscience."

Lucy frowned. "How convenient. You seem to insert God whenever needed."

"Maybe it's convenient because it's the best explanation," Jack answered gently.

"Still not convinced," Lucy stated.

Jack looked up, as if searching the clear blue sky for his next point. If it were not for their predicament, it would be a beautiful day. But the sun was hot, so the conversation was a good distraction.

Then Jack started to feel a little woozy and light-headed. He wondered if he was getting heatstroke. He took a gulp of water and swooshed it around in his mouth. He shook the thought of potential heatstroke and decided to press on.

"Is it possible for a society or country to make moral progress? To improve its laws and customs to become more good, in a certain sense?"

Peter jumped in. "Sure. Getting rid of slavery was a good thing. I would say that was moral progress."

"Exactly," Jack said, locking eyes with Peter and pointing at him. "How would it be possible to make moral improvement if society simply creates morality? It would not be possible. Neither society would be wrong."

"I still don't get it," Peter admitted.

"If societies really do make moral rules, then slavery could be okay for one society and then not for another. But we know this is absurd. It is contrary to our moral intuition. Slavery is wrong even if one society had deemed it okay. Consequently, the standard of goodness does not come from societies. It comes from God, and societies either move toward that standard or away from it.[38]"

Jack shook his head and swung his arms to and fro for emphasis. "Humankind does not set the rules for right and wrong—a source that transcends humankind—a.k.a. God—does!"

"Well if God makes the rules, why wouldn't He stop what just happened!" Lucy scowled. "Remember? Skipper stealing our food?"

"In other words, why is there evil?" Jack asked. "It's a fair question. If you were struggling emotionally I would simply try to be there for you. Listen. Pray. Like I tried to be there for Tad. But since you are asking an intellectual question, I will try to offer an explanation."

Jack tried to swallow, but his mouth was again parched. He knew they all needed to be getting more water. They still had a few bottles of rainwater, but they were rationing it. Dehydration and heatstroke were their biggest enemies right now. He felt the heat cooking his pink arms. They weren't quite as bad as his legs, but the damage was building. He took another sip of water to help him continue.

"Do you believe we all have free will?" Jack asked. "The ability to make good or bad choices?"

"Sure. But shouldn't God intervene when people do evil, like take our food?" Lucy countered.

"So ... if God were to allow only good acts and stop all evil acts, is that truly free will?" Jack responded. "I don't think so. For us to have true free will, God has to allow us to make good and bad decisions."[39]

"At our expense," Lucy said, folding her arms and turning away.

"Free will is extremely important. For God to have a genuine love relationship with His creation, He grants everyone the ability to choose to love Him and follow Him or rebel and go their own way."[40]

"I don't know," Lucy mumbled. She sounded unconvinced, but Jack knew that was the remark she tended to make when was slightly impressed.

"I'm hungry," Peter muttered, rubbing his stomach with his left hand. "Could really go for a candy bar." Peter's eyes narrowed, revealing an angry expression. "Can't believe he gave it to a dog. A dog!"

"Peter? Who is more valuable, you or the dog?" Jack asked, deciding to make a different point. He quickly followed his question with a gesture at Lucy, warning her not to take the opportunity to insult her brother.

A smile came over Peter's face. "Hmmm. Let me think," he joked.

Jack smirked at Peter's sense of humor. Then his facial expression turned serious again. "It's obvious that people are more valuable than dogs. And dogs are more valuable than ants. And ants are more valuable than rocks. The point is that our moral intuition tells us that there is a hierarchy of value in nature. This does not make sense with atheism. If atheism were true, then everything is simply a random collection of atoms, and therefore they have no real difference in intrinsic value.[41] Also, a hierarchy of value in nature does not make sense for any religions that believe that everything in the universe is connected and all part of one essence."[42]

Jack took a breath and then continued. "There is a difference between moral rules and moral values.[43] Killing the innocent is wrong, which is the rule, but the degree of wrongness is different when one kills a person versus an animal. Both are wrong, but our moral intuition tells us that killing an innocent human is worse. That is because there is clearly a difference in value among living things. Where does that hierarchy come from? It only makes sense if God exists. All of creation is valuable because God created it, people, dogs, cats, trees, and so on, but things that most closely resemble

56

God, such has humans made in God's image, are more valuable than others."[44]

"If we are so valuable, then why does God allow evil and suffering in the world!" Lucy shouted, releasing some frustration. "I have been asking you this same question for days, yet you still have not answered it. If people are valuable, why allow us to suffer!"

"I told you," Jack said tenderly. "God allows free will in creation to have a genuine love relationship. Adam and Eve rebelled against God, and now humankind is corrupted with an insatiable desire to satisfy self, which leads to sin. We are all still capable of doing good, but we are clearly not morally perfect. We all do wrong."

"Even if free will makes sense for evil that comes from people's bad decisions, it certainly doesn't explain natural evil," Lucy exclaimed. "Why does God allow cancer and other diseases? Why allow us to go through all of this?"

"What is God's number one priority for human beings?" Jack asked.

"How should I know?" Lucy snapped.

"Exactly," Jack answered, pointing at his daughter. Her eyes widened, as if taken back, wondering what she had said that agreed with his point.

Jack finished, "How can you condemn God for allowing suffering in the world if you don't know God's priority?"

"Because I would assume caring for His creation and making us happy would be most important," Lucy countered with sass.

"And that's where I think you're wrong," Jack said. "I don't think God's number one priority is to make us happy, rather knowing, loving, and trusting in God.[45] God wants us recognize our sin and choose to follow Him. God wants us to make the most important decision of our life with free will: turn from our selfishness and sin to accept Jesus as Lord and trust in Him as our Savior from the punishment we deserve for our sin."

"How does suffering do that?" Lucy asked snidely. "I would think people could do that without suffering."

"Would people pursue God if their lives were absolutely perfect? If they had everything they ever wanted? I tend to think otherwise. I think people are much more likely to pursue God when they recognize the brokenness of their lives; or perhaps the impact that sin has done to their relationship with their Creator. Although God does not desire us to suffer, He will allow it if there is ultimately a good reason that benefits our souls."

"How can you know that any specific suffering benefits our souls?" Peter chimed in with an unusual counter.

"We usually don't know. That's the challenge. And some situations of hardship may not even be intended to benefit us, but perhaps for someone else. God is omniscient, knowing everything. We have finite knowledge.[46] It's kind of like parents knowing what is best for their toddlers. The toddler has no idea what is best for them and needs to trust their parent."

"What does Christianity offer that I cannot get from being an atheist?" Lucy asked.

"A lot," Jack answered. "Hope. Eternal life. Truth. God is the best explanation for the evidence around us."

"Well of course," Lucy said in a sarcastic tone, not really believing the answer. "God is your solution for all tough questions."

"Lucy, I am not forcing a square peg into a round hole. God is the best explanation for the moral rules and values that exist. Why do you feel the need to force some naturalistic answer that doesn't fit? Are you open to God being the answer?"

Jack noticed something behind Lucy, far off in the distance. He tried to focus his eyes to make sure that it wasn't a false image, something his mind was creating because he desired it to be there.

Lucy opened her mouth but hesitated. She clearly noticed her dad looking past her. She whipped her head around. "What is it?"

Jack said softly, "I think I see land."

CHAPTER 5

"Dad!" Peter's voice was filled with panic. "What are you doing? You're not getting in the water, are you?"

Jack was leaning over the front edge of the raft, his right leg hanging off the side. He was face down toward the water examining the sandy ocean floor. He was trying to gauge how deep the water was—whether it was over his head. Although the water was fairly clear, it was difficult to determine the depth.

It was day seven in the raft, and they had drifted to within about forty feet from land. The morning sun had just risen. The pink sky revealed an inviting coastline. A small, sandy beach was followed by land filled with trees and hills. It was a welcomed sight after a week of drifting at sea.

Jack was desperate to get out and pull the raft to safety, not wanting to risk drifting backward. But he was still concerned about ocean predators, namely sharks. The horrible experience of losing his friend to a large sea creature had left a traumatic, deep scar that would not be forgotten.

Lucy was half awake. Although all three of them were hungry and thirsty, Jack was very concerned about her energy level, which seemed completely drained due to her rather slight body weight. She was pale and lethargic. She didn't even seem to have the strength to express any frustration. Jack missed that fiery energy from his youngest daughter.

The waves were strong compared to previous days. They pushed the raft forward, then backward, and for some time now, the raft seemed to be stuck at a stone's throw away from the shoreline, simply swaying to and fro. Jack's frustration was escalating. He wondered whether the tide was shifting, beginning to head back out to sea. They needed to get to land, and he didn't have the patience to wait any longer.

Jack flipped his legs over the edge of the raft, taking the plunge. He was able to stand, but the water level was up to his neck.

"Dad! Get back in!" Peter begged.

Jack ignored the request. Getting his footing on the mixture of sand and stones below, he began to pull the front of the raft toward the shore. The task was difficult at this depth. He didn't have much leverage. His right foot slipped out. A wave crashed over his head. He spit out some saltwater; swallowing would have accelerated his dehydration. He alternated between yanking the raft and trying to swim. Neither was very effective. Progress was slow.

As he continued to try to pull the raft, Jack had an uneasy feeling and spun his head around. He scanned the waters behind the raft, looking for shark fins. Nothing that he could see. *That doesn't mean danger isn't approaching from just below the surface,* he thought to himself.

He had never been this anxious about the ocean, but the recent experience of seeing a shark fin approaching, dip below the water, and then to have Tad's body ripped from his arms had left a mark on his psyche. But he refused to let that fear stop him from doing what he needed to do to help his family survive, such as when he had jumped into the ocean to gather the packaged food; unfortunately the horrible memory would likely never leave his mind. He would forever be concerned about the potential danger below.

Jack continued to strain to pull the raft to safety. He turned back to check the distance to the shoreline. They had moved slightly closer to land, but it was taking longer than he hoped.

A large splash of water behind Jack startled him. He felt sheer terror—fear that he was about to be attacked, bitten by sharp teeth.

He snapped his head around to see what caused the splash. For a moment, Jack was relieved to see that it was Peter who had jumped into the water, in front of the raft, to his backside. But his relief quickly turned to concern for Peter's safety.

"Peter! Get back in!" Jack ordered.

"Let's go," Peter said, ignoring the command.

Rather than taking time to argue, Jack decided it was better to focus on hurrying, dragging the raft to safety. With his son in the water, Jack yanked with even more urgency. Together they made good progress. Within minutes they were at waist-high water. Then knee high.

Jack gave a giant exhale, relieved to be away from the dangers of the sea. He and Peter finished pulling the front of the raft out of the water, onto a small beach. They stepped onto dark sand, which was wet from waves, and looked around.

"Where are we?" Peter asked in between deep breaths.

"Somewhere back in Brazil," Jack answered. He bent over and propped his left hand against his knee, also catching his breath. His lungs burned from rapid breathing, caused by a combination of working hard and rushing to get Peter out of the water.

There was only about twenty feet of sandy beach before a series of trees led into the rainforest of Brazil.

After gathering his breath and energy, Jack picked Lucy up and out of the raft. She was too weak to walk and too lethargic to resist his help. As he carried her, he felt the sting of the sunburn on his arms. Fortunately the burn had not worsened from day five, but it was still a solid first-degree burn. His legs had a couple bubbles, but he chose to ignore the pain.

As Jack carried Lucy into the beginning portion of the jungle, he hollered over this shoulder, "Peter. Bring the raft."

There was a nice patch of rocky ground in-between some trees, about a hundred feet from the coast. Jack sat Lucy on a large rock and surveyed the surroundings. Peter joined them, dropped the raft next to Lucy, and plopped himself on the edge.

Trees, soaked by a recent rain shower, surrounded them. They provided screening against the oppressive rays from the sun, protecting them from further damage to their skin. A smattering of bird noises echoed from all around. The humidity was heavy; it was so dense if felt as though the air had weight. About three hundred feet ahead, slightly to the right, through thick foliage, was a large hill and another hill behind that one. Jack estimated the height of the first hill to be about fifty feet. *Probably a good place to get a look around.*

"Should we try to go up there?" Peter asked, clearly noticing his dad observing the slope.

Jack looked down at Lucy. "I'd like to, but your sister is in no shape to move yet. And I don't want to leave her. We need to rest here and get hydrated. We all need our strength to move carefully through that thick foliage. Jaguars, snakes, black caiman alligators—there could be anything hiding in that dense patch of jungle. Let's settle here for now. Gather food. Hopefully build a fire."

Jack was tired. He thought about resting but decided to push forward. There was a lot of work to be done. "Lucy, stay here," he said as he began to walk toward a crop of trees. "Peter, I need your help."

Peter sighed out loud and forced himself to his feet. He shuffled along and then caught up to his father. The two of them walked a short ways from the rock Lucy was sitting on.

Jack stopped and examined the trees. "Peter, we need to gather a lot of wood. We need it for a fire and a platform to keep us off the ground. But we need to be very careful. Snakes. Spiders. Bullet ants. And that …" Jack said pointing to the left. About twenty feet away was a giant centipede feeding on a lizard. Although partially coiled, the centipede looked to be about twelve inches in length. The dead lizard was halfway inside the centipede, its legs and tail dangling in the air.

Jack kicked a branch on the ground in front of him. He kicked it again, before grabbing the end, dragging it from between bushes into the open, and flipping it over. "We need a lot of branches like this, but I want you to be very careful about where you step and what you grab. Kick and shake each branch like I just did to make sure there's nothing dangerous. Don't go too far into the rainforest, and don't go over there." Jack pointed at the dense portion of the jungle.

Peter looked in the direction his father was pointing. "Why? What do you think is over there?" The tone of his voice was a mixture of intrigue and a bit of anxiety.

"Were you listening before?" Jack asked with a little exasperation. He was annoyed but reminded himself that he needed to be patient and supportive. They were all trying to function under bad circumstances—dehydration, hunger, and oppressive heat. "Again, maybe nothing. But it's very dense. Something big or small could easily surprise us."

Jack carefully detached a giant leaf that had accumulated some of the recent rainwater. "Bring that branch," Jack said to Peter as he started to head back to Lucy.

He looked over his shoulder and noticed Peter examining the branch. *Good*, he thought. *He needs to be careful.* Then, obviously deciding it was okay, Peter slowly grabbed the end and started to walk back, following Jack.

As Jack carefully poured the water from the leaf into Lucy's mouth, Peter dropped the log and placed his hands on his hips. "We might be able to scrounge some rainwater, but what are we going to eat?" Peter asked, rubbing his stomach.

Jack pointed to the left at a crop of trees and bushes. "Bananas and mangoes. I'll gather some later, but we really need to get a fire started. It could take some time, and I'm sure there are too many predators around us not to have a fire. Go gather lots of wood. But be careful."

Peter turned and headed back to the tree line. Lucy attempted to stand, but Jack put his hand on her shoulder, stopping her from getting up. "You need to rest or you'll get worse."

"No way," she said. "I'm no weakling. I can do something."

"You're too weak from lack of nourishment."

"I can still do something. Gather some small wood for the fire." She pushed his hand aside and stood up. It was obvious she didn't have a lot of energy, but Jack knew her stubbornness would not let up. He decided to give in to her persistence.

"Okay. But stay around here. Gather small branches to help get the fire started. But if you feel dizzy or light-headed, sit down immediately." Jack began heading toward Peter. "Don't overdo it," he hollered back to her.

Jack, Lucy, and Peter worked diligently. Jack collected several long branches, which he used to build a platform about a foot off the ground. It wasn't perfect, but it was sturdy. The raft was placed on top of it for further protection from creepy crawlies. Next, he gathered a pile of fruit.

Lucy and Peter collected a large pile of firewood. Unfortunately, most of it was fairly wet, difficult for making a fire. But Jack found a few dry branches and broke them into smaller pieces. He used them to build a small lean-to campfire inside a group of large rocks he had gathered in a circle. Jack was no survival expert, but he had done his fair share of camping and wilderness adventures.

"Ready to light it?" Peter asked.

"Uhhh," Jack muttered, closely examining the little structure, trying to decide if it was ready. They only had five matches, so he needed to be cautious about how they were used. "I guess so. Probably as good as it's going to get."

"Please help us, God," Jack said out loud. Out of the corner of his vision, he could see Lucy roll her eyes.

Jack removed one of the matches from a waterproof case. He scraped it against a rock. Nothing. He did it again, and the friction removed most of the ignition contents off the top of the match. A third attempt snapped the stick in half; still no flame. It was clearly ruined, so Jack placed it on the campfire and grabbed another match. He repeated the process, this time against a different rock, hoping for a better result. It burst into flame, and Jack lit some small tinder inside the lean-to. It caught quickly, sending flames against tiny twigs as well as wooden carvings he had made with the pocketknife.

The flames built gradually. Soon they were hot enough to add a few bigger pieces. Jack let out a big sigh of relief. "Thank you, God," he said aloud.

Jack looked at the pile of wood they had gathered, which they had placed around the edge of the campfire to help it dry out. There was a fair amount of wood but not enough to stop Jack from worrying. *What if some pieces are just too wet? What if we run out of usable wood, especially at night? How would we keep predators away? Would we be fortunate enough to get another fired started? We can't lose this fire.*

"I think we need a few more pieces," Jack said in Peter's direction.

"You gotta be kidding," he replied. Peter looked quite fatigued.

"We can't be trying to gather firewood at night in the event that we run out," Jack replied, noticing that the sunlight was beginning to fade. The day had flown by. The sun was in its final descent. In less than an hour, the sunlight would be gone. Jack continued to attend the fire, progressively adding bigger kindling to the growing flames, trying to make sure it did not fizzle out. "Please get a few more pieces, just in case. I need to stay and make sure the fire does not go out."

Peter grunted and muttered some gibberish as he turned and headed back to the forest. He needed to go a little deeper toward the hill to try to find some wood on the ground. The descending sun provided a little less light. A veil of darkness started to cover the jungle. Trees provided lots of shadows. Branches swayed from a slight breeze.

Peter looked around and listened for noises from potential predators moving in the dense part of the jungle. There was a fair amount of action in the trees, which seemed to be birds flying from branch to branch. He got a pit in his stomach, wondering if he was being watched.

But there was nothing obvious.

Peter scanned a new area of the woods around him and located a log on the ground. It was fairly thick but short. *Should be able to drag that one*, he thought to himself.

Peter gave the log a couple of kicks and then flipped it over. His eyes grew wide. He froze with fear as a large Brazilian Wandering Spider sat on the ground three feet from him. Its long, dangly legs were brown and hairy; with them sprawled apart, the spider measured about six inches in diameter. It had eight black eyes just above its reddish jaw, which hid its dangerous fangs. His dad had warned him multiple times that this type of spider is one of the most venomous in the world and can be aggressive.

Peter hated spiders. Actually he was terrified of them. It was by far his worst fear. And now it was a reality.

Peter wanted to back up, but his legs weren't obeying his mind. He felt goose pimples popping out on his arms; the hair on back of his neck prickled sharply. He got chills. The spider was facing Peter but not moving.

Maybe it's sleeping, he wondered. He hoped.

Peter was finally able to lift his right foot and began to slowly move it backward. Suddenly, the spider lifted its four front legs and began to rock back and forth, a clear sign that the spider felt threatened by the movement. Peter felt the blood drain from his head and a massive pit in his stomach. He wanted to run but thought moving slowly still might be best. He placed his right foot on the ground and started to slowly take a step back with his left foot.

Suddenly the spider started aggressively charging forward. Peter spun and ran as fast as he could. Adrenaline filled his body. Sheer terror compelled him to run with urgency. He didn't dare look behind him.

As Peter was sprinting back to base camp, terrible thoughts ran through his mind. He feared that when he turned his back, the spider somehow ran onto his leg and was now racing up his back. Maybe it was closing in on his exposed neck. Maybe it had somehow run up his shorts or inside his loose shirt. Although unlikely, the possibilities were torturing his mind. He couldn't help but scream. "Ahhhhhh!"

Jack heard Peter yelling and turned to see him running from the jungle.

"What?" Jack yelled, frantically looking around to see what might be following Peter. He began running to his son.

They reached each other in seconds, and Peter spun around. "Sp-spider," he muttered between deep, panting breaths. "Anything ... my back." He pointed behind himself with his thumb.

Jack scanned Peter quickly. "Nothing," he said, relieved that there wasn't a larger predator chasing him. "You saw a Brazilian Wandering Spider, didn't you?" Jack lifted Peter's shirt and tapped all around his clothes, still not finding anything.

With obvious relief, Peter placed his hands on his knees and leaned over. He began to let out a large exhale, but it turned into a dry heave. Chills from fear caused him to vomit, but with no contents in his stomach, only a string of saliva came out.

Peter nodded and pointed his right index finger toward the wood they had gathered throughout the day. "I think we have enough wood for tonight ... for tomorrow ... and the day after."

Jack smirked at Peter's joke—or at least he hoped it was a joke.

CHAPTER 6

Over the next hour, the sun disappeared, along with its rays of light. Visibility faded quickly. Clouds hid the celestial lights, so it was very dark. The large flames of the campfire were their only source of illumination. It also produced some level of warmth to counter the cool ocean winds that had picked up, and it provided a sense of protection from potential predators.

The sounds of the jungle had come alive. They were louder than anything the family had previously heard when living in the Brazilian village. These sounds were eerie. They popped out from all directions, hidden in the darkness of the night. Loud noises from insects. Squawking birds. Periodic movement in the jungle foliage. Crunching leaves. Moving branches. Each sound caused Jack's imagination to run wild with what could be creeping around just a short distance away.

Jack continued to sharpen a weapon. He used the pocketknife to shave the head of a sturdy, five-foot pole, making a spear. He examined the point, wondering how well it would work against predators. Would it be able to penetrate the tough armor of an alligator? Would it pierce the scaly skin of a large snake? He shook the questions from his mind, choosing to be optimistic about his new weapon.

Jack looked up at his teenage children. Lucy had just finished chewing the last bite of a mango as Peter was nearing the end of his third banana. Jack recalled the fresh taste of the fruit. The mangoes were juicy. The bananas provided substance to fill his grumbling stomach. But he wisely chose to pace himself, worrying that if he overate and vomited he would lose water he couldn't afford to be without.

"Why don't you both get some sleep?" Jack said. "I'll take first watch and then wake one of you." He was exhausted but knew he wouldn't be able to fall asleep for a while. A few times when his body began to settle and his eyes grew tired, some movement in the trees or rustling leaves snapped him back to readiness, his body getting a jot of adrenaline, expecting the worst.

Lucy and Peter didn't argue. They discarded the remnants of the fruit they had eaten by tossing them far into the darkness. They each picked a side in the raft, which rested on the wooden platform they had built.

Jack finished sharpening his weapon. He scanned the jungle. Light from the flickering fire danced against the trees and bushes. He couldn't discern if the jungle was moving or if it was simply the fire. His mind started to see things that may or may not be there. Movement of branches. Slithering on the ground. Faces of birds and reptiles.

He focused on an object on the ground several feet away. It was either the end of a large stick or the head of snake, staring at him. He watched for movement. The flickering flames made it difficult. He convinced himself it was simply a stick, but he couldn't take his eyes off of it, just in case he was wrong.

After a few minutes of stillness, Lucy spoke, interrupting Jack's imagination.

"Feels weird," she said.

"What?" Jack asked.

"Lying in the raft while it's not moving in the water," Peter interjected, apparently experiencing the same sensation.

Jack didn't respond. He let his thoughts drift back to the previous questions he was wrestling with earlier in the day. *What should we do next? What is the right course of action? Should we stay where we are, away from civilization where the disease could be spreading? Should we travel inland, seeking food and other resources? Should we try to find help and a new way to get home or stay away from civilization for the time being?*

Jack really didn't know what was best. Each time he started to consider one course of action as the best, a new concern entered his mind and raised some doubt. He wasn't afraid for himself, but he was for his children.

Lucy and Peter took turns repositioning themselves on their respective sides, trying to get comfortable. After a short time, Jack realized neither of them were sleeping.

"Close your eyes and think of good things," Jack said, a phrase he had been telling them since they were small children. It seemed far more awkward to say now, given all that had happened to them over the past week.

"I closed my eyes a few minutes ago, and all I could think of was spiders crawling on me," Lucy grumbled. "Kinda hard to think of good things."

"That's weird," Peter jumped in. "I closed my eyes and thought of spiders crawling on you too." He chuckled at his own joke.

"The sounds around us are freaky," Lucy said, apparently ignoring her brother's comment and referring to something more important to her.

Jack grimaced, wondering how he could get their attention off the worries of the jungle so that they could sleep at some point. Then an idea popped into his mind, *Get Lucy debating, which always seems to distract her and settle her nerves.* He had wanted to return to the topic of religion at the right time anyway. This might be a good way to take her mind off the jungle, maybe prevent dangerous images from popping into her mind.

"Fortunately we have this fire," Jack said. "It is the only light we have on a very dark night. We would be in terrible danger without it. It reminds me of Jesus, who is the light for this dark world, and we would be in terrible danger without Him."

Jack's idea was right on. The mention of religion clearly grabbed Lucy's attention. "Really, Dad? You're going to talk about Jesus now? And doing so with a rather odd illustration?"

"Making an observation," Jack answered. "The world is a dark place. Literally dark for us right now, but also figuratively dark due to all the evil, pain, and suffering. But no matter what our circumstances are, we can always take comfort in the fact that God cares about us. He came in the form of a man, Jesus, to teach us truth, and He went to the cross to take the punishment of our sins. No matter what happens in our short lives on earth, His followers will be with Him in heaven forever. We can trust Jesus. He claimed to be God and proved He is God."

"God? I don't think so," Lucy retorted. "Jesus was just a man like everyone else. Maybe a good teacher. Maybe. But a god? I don't think so. Jesus was no different than every other religious founder. Someone who spewed some stuff about morality and got a bunch of people to follow Him."

Jack's plan seemed to be working. Lucy naturally enjoyed arguing. Unlike many people who try to avoid verbal conflict, it seemed to be her comfort zone.

"Jesus claimed to be God," Jack countered. "How could He be a good teacher if He lied about His identity?"[47]

"So you say," Lucy said, extending an arm outside of the raft and pointing at her father. She was still lying down, alongside Peter, who had yet to speak. "But how do we really know that? How do we really know that Jesus claimed to be God? Maybe that is just some legend that developed over time. Huh?"

"There's no question Jesus claimed to be God. You know that." Jack's tone was gentle but confident. He was surprised at Lucy's remark, as this was not the first time they had had this conversation. But it was the first time she was questioning the claim.

"No. I don't know that," Lucy said nonchalantly. "And neither do you."

"Well let's refresh our memories."

"Go ahead," Lucy answered, "and I will tell you why you are wrong. You know I have been reading about some alternatives."

"Yeah, but you know better than to trust everything you read on the internet, my little girl," Jack responded. "Little girl" was his term of endearment for his youngest daughter. "Just because you read about some alternatives on the internet, that doesn't make them true. You know better, Lucy. We need to know the reasons behind the claim."

"Little girl?" Lucy snickered. "When I was little, you could tell me things and I would believe them. But now I need reasons, Dad. You can't simply tell me what to believe."

Little girl. Hearing Lucy say it caused Jack's thoughts to drift back to a time ten years ago when Lucy was six years old. He was teaching her to ride a bike. She wasn't as independent back then, and her Dad was her hero. She didn't mind being Daddy's little girl. She trusted everything he told her. But now she liked to challenge him. Ironically, debating and challenging conventional thinking was a trait she probably got from him.

"Want some examples?" Jack asked, knowing the response he would get.

Before Lucy answered, Peter chimed in. "You're wasting your breath, Dad. Lucy's not going to change her mind." He let out a large yawn. "She just likes to argue."

"You're so ignorant, Peter," Lucy snapped. "You just believe everything you're told. Yeah, Dad, try to convince me. But be prepared for a rebuttal. I am not as sleepy as my dim-witted brother."

Jack noticed an increase in light descending from the sky. He looked up to see that an opening in the clouds revealed a near-full moon. Virtually no stars were visible, but the moon was peeking through.

He quickly snapped back to the discussion. "According to the Bible, Jesus clearly claimed to be God. Let me start with one good example. After Jesus was arrested, the Jewish high priest questioned Jesus about whether He was the Son of God. Jesus answered in the affirmative, while referencing a prophecy from the book of Daniel that pertained to the Messiah."[48]

"Aren't we all supposed to be children of God?" Lucy interrupted.

"Jesus's claim about Himself was clearly different, as He referenced an Old Testament prophecy about the Messiah who is to be worshipped. Also, we can tell what Jesus meant by the reaction of the high priest; he accused Jesus of blasphemy, which is claiming to be God. He then condemned Jesus to death. The accusation of blasphemy makes it obvious that the high priest knew exactly what Jesus was claiming."

"Meh. One verse?" Lucy said, clearly unimpressed.

Jack was about to continue when he felt something crawling up the side of his leg. It had multiple legs and felt like quite large. He immediately slapped it off. His fingers didn't touch the body, but connected with several legs that felt a little hairy. *That was not a small insect*, he thought. His mind considered some alternatives. *It could have been a goliath bird-eating tarantula. Or maybe I was mistaken about the hairy legs and it was some sort of large beetle, such as a longhorn beetle.*

Dangerous insects that crawled around the Amazon rainforest were a big concern. Fortunately Jack had thought of this possibility for the raft. He had placed hot stones that had been in the fire around the four posts of the platform that held the raft. The hot stones prevented any dangerous critters from trying to get in the raft. But it was some work to rotate in new rocks when they cooled.

However, for the person keeping watch, they were more exposed to snakes, spiders and other insects and needed to be alert.

Rather than worry about what it might have been, Jack chose to press on, resuming the discussion, "In another account of the New Testament, Jesus claimed to exist before Abraham from the Old Testament, who lived hundreds of years before Jesus was born. In other words, that wouldn't be possible if Jesus was an ordinary man. Rather, Jesus was claiming to exist prior to Abraham. And in the same account, Jesus took the name 'I AM,' which is God's name from the Old Testament.[49] Again, Jesus was clearly claiming to be God; the crowd picked up stones to stone Him, which is a reaction to blasphemy, a serious issue in first-century Palestine."

"Not impressed," Lucy quipped. "Maybe all these claims developed after Jesus's early followers died."

"No. Jesus's disciples also claimed He was God, including the apostles Peter, Paul, and John, pillars of the early Christian church.[50] Not only that, Jesus did things that only God would do, actions that are only permitted by God Himself."[51]

"Wait," Lucy said, sitting up in the raft. "What did you say? Actions Jesus did … that only God would do?" She sounded puzzled; the expression on her face matched her tone.

Her reaction surprised Jack. *Is she genuinely interested? She seems to be.* "Absolutely. One example is that Jesus forgave sins, something the Bible says only God can do. In the gospel of Mark, Jesus healed a paralytic and also forgave his sins. The Jewish leaders with them wondered, 'Who can forgive sins but God Himself?'[52] Forgiveness is something that no other person in the Bible did—again, because only God can do so."

"I don't know," Lucy said, apparently trying not to show agreement. She lay back down in the raft.

Jack continued. "Also, Jesus accepted worship.[53] This is a serious action that according to Jewish belief can only be directed to God. Even Jesus said that only God is to be worshiped.[54] If Jesus did not believe He was God, He would have stopped people from worshiping Him. But He didn't do that."

"How do we know Jesus really accepted worship?" Lucy countered. "Isn't it more likely that the authors lied about that?"

"No. There are multiple things I could say, but one reason I don't believe the authors lied is based on a specific account about worship that has an embarrassing detail. When Jesus appeared after the resurrection, one Bible account mentions that the disciples worshiped Him, but some doubted.[55] The mention of doubt makes sense since someone rising from the dead is obviously a miracle. At the same time, doubt is an embarrassing detail that would not have been included if the author was lying."

"Hmm," Lucy grunted.

Not too much of a reaction, Jack thought. *Perhaps Lucy is getting tired or just being dismissive, not knowing how else to respond. Keep going. Either she'll fall asleep or consider some of the points.*

"I'll give you one more," Jack continued. "The apostle John writes that Jesus created everything that was ever created.[56] If Jesus made everything that was ever created, then He cannot have been created because He cannot create Himself. Consequently, if Jesus was not created, He must be God."

"Dad, stop!" Lucy snapped back, apparently more awake than Jack realized. "You're referencing everything from the Bible. You know I don't believe the Bible is true. It was written by a bunch of men to control people."

"Why do you believe that?" asked Jack.

"I just do," answered Lucy. "People were hungry for power, and before people started to think for themselves, the religious nuts of the day used the concept of God to control people."

"Again, you're making an assertion. I love you and your passion, but do you have any reasons to support these claims?"

"It's my opinion," Lucy responded.

"I'm glad you recognize it's your opinion. My belief is that the Bible is reliable, true, and inspired by God. But it's not just an opinion—it is my belief based on good reasons."

"What reasons?" Lucy snapped. "Grandpa said so?" Her tone tailed off as if worried she may be crossing a line by mentioning her grandfather.

Jack was surprised by the verbal jab but chose to ignore it and proceed. He didn't want to get emotional. "I have good reasons to believe the Bible is historically reliable and true, and it is not just a book written by man, but it is the very Word of God."

"Like I said, what reasons?" Lucy pushed. "If you are going to ask me for reasons for my opinion, then I will do the same to you. How do you know the Bible hasn't changed over the centuries?"

Jack felt a bite on the side of his neck. It started as an annoyance but then quickly became a sharp pain, like a needle penetrating his skin. He smacked his neck, crushing something small in his hand. He looked at his hand and through the faint campfire light saw small crumpled legs. He wondered if it was a mosquito but then dismissed that idea considering the sharpness of the pain. It was not painful enough to be a bullet ant, whose bite actually feels like a gunshot wound, but it certainly hurt. He rubbed his arms and legs to make sure there weren't any ants crawling on his flesh.

He rolled the small log he was sitting on closer to the fire, hoping that being uncomfortably close to the fire and smoke would prevent further creepy crawlies from attacking him. Again, he chose to press on with the discussion.

"There are a total of sixty-six books in the entire Bible. Let's talk specifically about the twenty-seven New Testament books. Although we don't have the original writings, we have thousands of copies, including some dated within a relatively short time from the original."[57]

"But I've heard there are lots of differences or errors between the copies. How do you know that what we have today is the same as the original?" Lucy asked.

Jack was surprised she knew about some differences in the manuscripts. He wondered if she had gotten that from friends or the internet. *Probably the latter,* he concluded.

"It's a fair question, but there's a good answer. There are some variations among the copies, but the vast majority are quite minor, like misspellings.[58] More importantly, scholars use the numerous copies to crosscheck all of them and determine the original writing. A manuscript with a different letter or word stands out as incorrect when compared to numerous other copies. Also, we can have confidence in the manuscripts because of how close they are dated to the original writing. These manuscripts are early, much closer to the original writing in comparison to other ancient documents, such as Homer's *Iliad*."[59]

"Who cares?" Lucy said snidely, conceding that point. "Suppose what we have today is the original content. How do we know they told the truth? Isn't it more likely they lied? Made all this stuff up, like I said to control people?" She added air quotes around the word *control*. "If I had to guess, that is what I think happened."

"Again, you make an assertion, but do you have any reasons to believe they made this up?" asked Jack. "It's quite easy to throw out these theories, but what are your reasons? I push you because I love you and want you to follow the truth."

"Unless, you have some good reasons to believe they told the truth, I think they probably lied. The world is filled with all these different religions. So, barring some good reasons, I think I'm justified in my skepticism."

Jack felt a cool breeze coming from the ocean. It was even colder now. The wind was biting at the back of his sunburnt neck that was facing away from the fire. It reminded him of the cold nights while they were adrift at sea.

"Not sure that conclusion follows, but let's move forward," Jack said. "I'll give you three main reasons why I trust that the authors of the Bible told the truth. First, the Bible includes numerous *embarrassing details* that the authors would not have included if they were making up all these stories. We're talking about important people in the Bible. Adam and Even rebelled against God and tried to pass the blame.[60] Noah got drunk.[61] David committed adultery and then had the husband murdered.[62] Peter was rebuked by Jesus. He was a key leader in the early church, and at one point Jesus called him Satan because Peter was focused on man's concerns instead of God's.[63] Paul was one of the worst sinners before becoming a believer, persecuting the church and approving Christians going to jail or death.[64] I could go on, but the point is that embarrassing details are a strong reason to believe that the authors told the truth.

The Bible does not hide embarrassing details about key figures but rather records the accounts as they occurred."

"Meh." Lucy grimaced. "I'm not convinced. So what? A bunch of men did immoral things. What else is new?"

"Hmmm. I think embarrassing details is a strong argument that the authors of the Bible told the truth." Jack rubbed his chin with a thumb and index finger. Over the past week, the hair on his face had grown into a small beard and mustache. "But I can't force you to be persuaded by what I find convincing. I just ask that you keep an open mind."

"I'm open," Lucy stated. "I'm open. But not easily convinced."

"Okay. Reason number two. Jesus's disciples were willing to die for their beliefs."

Lucy interrupted, "A lot of people are willing to die for what they believe in."

"Yes, many people are willing to die for what they believe, but virtually no one is willing to die for what they know is a lie.[65] The disciples would have known whether their claims to have seen the risen Jesus were true. And they would not all be willing to throw away their belief system and put their lives in danger if they knew the claim was false. We have historical evidence that indicates Jesus's disciples were willing to die for their claims.[66] There is no historical record of any of Jesus's disciples recanting."

Jack heard a loud buzzing sound near his left ear. It was much louder than a mosquito; he hesitated from swatting at it in case it was something dangerous. His first thought was it could be a tarantula hawk wasp, a giant flying insect that delivers an excruciating sting. He jerked his head away from the buzzing sound and it seemed to fly off. He exhaled a sigh of relief.

I don't know what that was, but glad it's gone, he thought. He shifted a little closer to the fire for protection. He then placed a few more dry green leaves on the flames to generate more smoke to protect them all from the flying insects.

"And number three?" Lucy asked, as if not yet persuaded by anything her father had said.

"Number three. There are good reasons to believe that the Bible is the inspired Word of God—not just a book written by people but also inspired by God Himself."

"Whoa. Quite the claim, Dad. Do tell," Lucy said sarcastically. She closed her eyes and folded her hands over her stomach.

"The Bible was written by more than forty different authors over a period of about fifteen hundred years, yet has one ultimate theme—God's plan of salvation for humankind.[67] Through the sixty-six different books, the Bible gives an account of the rebellion of humankind, their predicament of a broken relationship with their Creator, an impending judgment for breaking God's rules, and then God initiating a rescue plan[68] through Abraham and the Israelites, which eventually culminated in the life and sacrifice of God's Son, Jesus, for all humanity. Whoever puts their trust in Him, His sacrifice pays for that individual's sins, and their relationship with God is restored."

"Sounds like a fairy tale," Lucy muttered.

"But how could this so-called fairy tale be written through numerous different books of the Bible, gradually over centuries by so many different people, yet come together in *one cohesive story*?" Jack asked tenderly. "Isn't it more likely it was by the direction of a divine Author guiding prophets to record certain content?"

Not waiting for a response, Jack continued. "But perhaps the strongest argument that God guided the authorship of the Bible is prophecy."

"Like predicting the future?" Lucy asked, again with a sarcastic tone. This one included some hints of drowsiness, as if Lucy was feeling more comfortable and may actually, at some point, fall asleep.

"Yes. The Bible has hundreds of prophecies,[69] predictions about the future. About half of them have not happened yet[70] because they pertain to the end of the world. But there are hundreds of prophecies that have occurred. There is no way human beings could have known and written them before they happened. Only God truly knows the future."[71]

"You're naïve, Dad. Don't you think it's more likely that some things happened and then people wrote them down, lying about them being a prediction?"

"No I don't. And I can prove it to you," Jack answered Lucy without hesitation. "The Old Testament, which has thirty-nine books, contains numerous prophecies about the Messiah who would come into the world. Historians have confirmed the Old Testament was clearly written before Jesus was born.[72] So they couldn't have written the prophecies after Jesus fulfilled them. Even though it is mathematically impossible for one person to fulfill all of the prophecies,[73] Jesus does. That says something about both the Bible and Jesus."

"It says something about you," Lucy quipped. "You're more easily convinced than I am. Couldn't Jesus just go around and do all the things that were predicted and then claim to be the Messiah?"

"No. Some prophecies were out of his control."

"Such as?"

"The prophecy that the Messiah would be born in Bethlehem.[74] Jesus had no control over that."

Lucy grimaced.

"The prediction that the Messiah would suffer and die with His hands and feet being pierced.[75] Doesn't this sound like a crucifixion? This was predicted about a thousand years before Jesus was born[76] and quite possibly before crucifixion was even invented."[77]

Lucy nodded her head backward, as if the words actually struck her forehead, perhaps impressed by that point.

"Also, there are numerous prophecies about the genealogy of the Messiah coming from a certain line of descendants, including Abraham, Isaac, Jacob, and David.[78] Jesus fulfills all of them. Again, He could not have forced the fulfillment of His lineage."

Jack continued. "These numerous prophecies about who the Messiah would be and what He would do are all fulfilled by Jesus.

Again, that has to say something about the Bible and the person of Jesus."

Lucy shrugged her shoulders.

"But one of my favorites is an event in the Old Testament, well before Jesus was born.

"When the Israelites grumbled against God, they were punished with poisonous snakes, which represent sin. God told Moses to hang a snake on a pole, and anyone who looked at the pole would be healed. "The Lord said to Moses, 'Make a snake and put it up on a pole; anyone who is bitten can look at it and live.' So Moses made a bronze snake and put it up on a pole. Then when anyone was bitten by a snake and looked at the bronze snake, they lived."[79][80]

"There is no way Moses could have known that this event was going to foreshadow Jesus being crucified on a cross. Hundreds of years later, Jesus referred to this event about Himself as the means of salvation. 'Just as Moses lifted up the snake in the wilderness, so the Son of Man must be lifted up, that everyone who believes may have eternal life in him.'[81][82]

"The best explanation for this extraordinary foreshadowing of Jesus's crucifixion is that God inspired the Bible."[83]

"That's actually pretty cool," Peter mumbled in a faint, groggy tone. He was obviously getting tired but clearly heard the point.

"I don't know …" Lucy let out a giant yawn, interrupting her words.

The conversation fizzled quickly, and soon both Lucy and Peter were asleep.

Jack's eyes were very heavy. He fought to keep them open. It had been a few hours since the teens fell asleep. For the first couple of hours, it was rather easy to stay alert. The eerie sounds of the jungle continued. They were particularly noisy from the dense portion— wild birds screeching, insects making odds sounds, and rustling leaves signaling movement. Something else sounded like a monkey shrieking, but he wasn't sure.

Even when Jack comforted himself about the noises, his thoughts haunted him. Although an insect had not bitten him in a while, the lack of visibility allowed his mind to imagine the horrors that may be crawling around his feet. Maybe up his back. Deadly spiders. Giant centipedes. Bullet ants.

Eventually the worries of the jungle began to fade. They were being overtaken by Jack's drowsiness. There is only so much action and stress a person can take until they succumb to sleep.

Since Lucy's energy was the most depleted, he would let her sleep longer. Peter would need to take second watch for a couple hours.

Jack wanted to stand up and make his way over to the raft and wake his son. But his tired body refused to obey his mind.

A few more minutes of sitting and gathering energy, he granted himself.

As he gazed into the blackness of the jungle, he came upon two faint circles of light about ten feet up in a tree, maybe thirty feet away. Two eyes—at least that is what they appeared to be—were gazing directly at him. Jack rubbed his eyes and strained them into focus. It was very dark, making it difficult to determine exactly what it was.

They really looked like two large eyes, evenly separated, staring down from a large branch. Again, his mind played with his emotions, imagining a terrible predator sitting up in the tree, stalking his family. Maybe a jaguar.

Jack grabbed his spear and watched intently for any movement. Nothing. The eyes just stayed in place. No moving. No blinking.

After a few minutes, Jack began to console himself. *It's nothing. You're imagining things. Lack of sleep will do that.*

His eyes had dried out from staring intently at the dark scenery. He rubbed them so that moisture would comfort the dryness.

But when Jack looked back up in the tree, the large eyes were gone. His body snapped to alertness and scanned his surroundings.

Nothing noticeable yet.

He imagined a predator sneaking toward them, hidden in the

shadows beyond the flickering light from the campfire. He looked back up in the tree. Again, no eyes.

He clenched his spear tightly, readying himself to fight. He was thankful for the fire but couldn't fully depend on it to protect them. He listened very carefully, awaiting any indication that something was approaching—the crunch of a leaf, snap of a twig, movement of a branch, anything.

Jack was very tense. His heart was beating strongly. His arms and neck were moist from sweat. He prayed in his mind, asking God for protection.

The loud sounds of the jungle were maddening. They made listening for a predator impossible. His mind imagined a jaguar stalking from behind, ready to pounce on him and bite his neck. Terror ran through his body like electricity. The hair on the back of his neck stood up. His head swiveled all around to see if something was approaching from the side or behind. Still nothing. He continued to stay alert.

But soon, seconds turned to minutes. Jack's heartbeat gradually eased. But his tension would not fully leave him until hours later when the first signs of daylight appeared. Only then would he wake Peter to allow himself a couple hours of sleep.

"Feeling better?" Jack asked as Lucy's eyes cracked open. It was clearly daylight.

She sat up and released a stretch. "Better," she muttered. "Between the fruit and sleeping, I feel much better. Did you sleep?" She was surprisingly in a pretty good mood, although she had always been a bit of a morning person, unlike her younger brother.

"Very little," Jack said with a yawn.

"Why not?"

"I need to tell you something that I already warned Peter about."

She looked to the side of the raft where Peter had slept and noticed it was empty. "Where is Peter?" she asked as her head swiveled around.

"Gathering food," Jack replied with a gesture toward the fruit trees that were in an open, visible area to the side that looked safe. "I told him to be careful but decided not to mention spiders. Figured he might not go otherwise."

"Oh. Is that the warning?" Lucy asked in a sleepy, unconcerned manner.

"No. Listen," Jack said with seriousness. "Some time last night, hours after you both fell asleep, I noticed something up in that tree." Jack pointed to a large tree about thirty feet away.

"Noticed something?" Lucy asked, with a tone indicating a little more interest.

"I don't want to scare you." Jack paused. "Actually I do. I need to warn you. I saw two eyes."

"Two eyes?" Lucy interrupted.

"I wasn't sure at the time, but yes two eyes, glimmering in the moonlight. They sat there, right on that large branch." He pointed. "I stared back at them for a while. I kept telling myself, *It's your imagination. It's something else that only looks like eyes.* Eventually, they disappeared."

"Disappeared?"

"Yeah. I guess I blinked or something and then they were just gone. I tried to dismiss it. But my curiosity got to me this morning. So I crept over to the tree at daylight and noticed large, fresh claw marks on the tree trunk."

Lucy looked puzzled, clearly trying to figure it out.

"A jaguar. No doubt about it," Jack said. "And probably a big one. I don't know if it wasn't hungry or the fire kept it away, but we're not staying here another night to find out."

"Where do we go?" Lucy asked. "What's the plan?"

"I wanted to go up that hill and get a look around. But that is right through the thick foliage where the jaguar may reside. I think we may try to go right and hug the coastline. See if there is an opening toward the mainland that looks friendly."

Peter wandered over with an arm full of bananas. "Mornin', Sis." He smiled in Lucy's direction.

"What have you been doing?" she asked. "Nothing important, I'm sure."

"Actually, important stuff. Gathering fruit, as you can see. That was after hunting jaguars with my keen intellect," Peter joked.

"And you're still alive? That's surprising," Lucy teased.

Suddenly the ground rumbled. The movement was small but noticeable. The sensation of the earth moving felt odd to Jack.

"Whoa," Peter said.

"What was that?" Lucy asked.

Jack looked at Lucy, then Peter. "That's the third one," he said with a puzzled tone. "There were two others last night—very slight. That one was definitely a little bigger."

"Earthquake?" Peter asked.

"Just small tremors. But maybe a sign for a coming earthquake. Remember the reports from around the world that they are more frequent since the bombings in Africa." Jack shook his head. "I don't know. Not something we can control."

"What's the plan?" Peter asked.

"We need to get away from here. Move farther inland. I think we may go that way," Jack said, pointing to the right.

"What about D6? We can't go to a town, right?" Lucy asked.

"D6?" Peter asked, as if he had never heard of it.

"Hello? Worldwide disease? Apocalypse," Lucy snapped. "Did the crash damage your brain?"

"I don't know about a town," Jack answered. "But I want to move away from this location."

Suddenly, the ground shook violently. Jack struggled to stay on his feet, while Peter stumbled to the ground, dropping the bananas to catch himself with his hands. It went on for about fifteen seconds, clearly a major earthquake.

Jack scanned the environment. Oddly there were few signs of wildlife. He wondered if they have already evacuated the area.

"Stay here. Next to the fire," Jack said. He grabbed the binoculars and began to jog toward the coast. He made it about halfway, then stopped and looked between the trees, putting his right hand to his forehead to shield the sun from his eyes. He then looked through the binoculars. After a few seconds, Jack realized he was seeing an enormous wall of water. He turned and sprinted back toward Lucy and Peter. He wasn't simply jogging back; he was running as fast as he could.

"What is it?" Lucy yelled to her father before he was all the way back.

Jack didn't respond. He was processing what to do next. *Where do we go?*

Jack arrived in seconds. "Lucy! Get your sneakers on! We need to go!" He quickly started throwing their few survival items in the backpack. His mind was still rapidly processing potential options.

"What is it!" Lucy demanded with panic.

"Tsunami! Huge! It's fairly far out at sea, but definitely coming this way. Earthquake must have been somewhere in the ocean floor. This place is going to be flooded."

Jack noticed Lucy and Peter look between the trees.

"I don't see anything," Peter said.

"Let's go!" Jack ordered, clipping the backpack shut.

"Where?" Lucy asked.

Jack grabbed his sharp spear and pointed at the hill. "Through the jungle foliage and up the hill."

"What about the jaguar?" Peter reminded.

"We have no choice with the tsunami coming," Jack responded. "Stay close to me. Hurry!" He turned and ran for the hill with the backpack strapped around his back and spear in hand.

Lucy and Peter followed closely. They ran with urgency toward the dense jungle, and Jack wondered if they would make high ground before the huge wall of seawater arrived.

CHAPTER 7

Jack, Lucy, and Peter reached the thick jungle in seconds. They wasted no time entering—Jack first, Lucy second, Peter third. Trees with large green leaves were crowded together, accompanied by bushes and long grass. With his left arm, Jack pushed branches to the side, clearing a way to walk. Some of the leaves were moist to the touch. With his right arm he readied the spear.

As they quickly proceeded, Jack periodically poked the heavy vegetation in front, checking for predators. The foliage was far too dense to jog, but they moved as swiftly as they could. Other than a few squawking birds, the jungle was much quieter than the eerie sounds at night but definitely not safe.

Just ten feet into the dense jungle, Jack jerked backward. He saw a green viper snake, coiled around a branch, head-level, about eighteen inches from his face. The color of the snake matched the green leaves around it. Jack was surprised he noticed it as it blended perfectly with the lush scenery. As he stopped, his movement caused branches to swing, angering the snake. Its head rose to striking position. The snake's mouth widened, showing its large fangs. Fortunately there were a few branches between Jack and the snake, continuing to swing back and forth, providing a partial shield from attack.

Jack extended his left arm to the side, blocking Lucy or Peter from trying to go around him.

"What is it?" Lucy asked, bumping into her father.

"Snake. Back up," Jack answered, as he started to backpedal.

They all stepped back a few feet and proceeded to the left, about five feet away from the dangerous snake.

After several steps Jack hesitated for a second as a branch startled a large bird in front of them. It flapped its wings through the trees, making a bunch of racket, and headed for a higher limb. Jack gave a noticeable sigh of relief, grateful that it wasn't something else.

They continued to move. He visualized the giant tsunami he had seen, and it brought back a sense of urgency. He picked up the pace. "Hurry! Stay with me!"

They made good progress, pushing through the dense branches. Jack wondered what dangerous predators were next to them or just in front, but they needed to keep moving. A different danger was closing in.

Halfway through the jungle, Lucy screamed. Jack spun around to see her looking at her shirt. A bright blue poison dart frog clung to her shirt. It was only about an inch long.

"Don't touch it," Jack said. He knew that just touching it could trigger sickness or possibly death.

"What is it?" Peter asked from behind his sister.

"Poison dart frog," Jack answered as he raised his staff. He easily knocked it off Lucy.

"Turn around," Jack said. Lucy didn't hesitate.

Jack's eyes scanned from bottom to top. He was just about to conclude everything was fine, when he noticed another poison dart frog just below her left shoulder. It was close to her hair and Jack worried it may jump inside.

"Don't move, Lucy."

"What?" she asked with panic.

Jack raised his staff and smacked it away. He quickly checked Peter. When he found nothing, they resumed their movement with urgency.

As they approached the end of the patch of jungle, just before the beginning of the rocky hill, Jack stopped sharply.

"Stop," he whispered, raising his arms to block passage around him.

Less than ten feet in front of them, slightly to the left, a large black caiman alligator sat, mostly hidden in some marsh. Jack couldn't see the entire alligator as its body and tail extended into tall grass, but based on the head and front section that was visible, Jack knew it was massive. *A gigantic monster*, he thought to himself.

"Oh my goodness," Lucy whispered from just behind her father.

"Don't move yet," Jack ordered as he examined the huge predator. It wasn't moving. Yet. But if it suddenly charged, it would be on them before they could react.

"Step back slowly," Jack said. "No sudden movements."

Suddenly the alligator's mouth opened and then snapped shut. The movement was fast and startling, too quick to react to, but Jack saw something inside the alligator's mouth. It looked like the wing of a large bird in its throat. Jack concluded they might be lucky that it was currently chewing on a meal and it might not be interested in them.

They slowly backed away. As the branches and grass hid the giant monster, Jack listened for movement in case the alligator charged them, aiming his spear in front, just in case. After several steps, they started to proceed to the far right of the alligator, but still heading for the hill. Jack moved with caution and shielded himself between the direction of the alligator and his children.

As they finally exited the jungle, the fear of the tsunami again consumed Jack's thoughts. *It must be getting close.*

"Let's go! Hurry!" Jack ordered.

They began sprinting up the steep slope. It was mainly sand and rock with a few patches of grass. Within seconds they were breathing heavy.

"Don't stop!" Jack ordered.

"Where are we going?" Peter asked as he took the lead.

"Just get up the hill," Jack answered, beginning to pant. He was already starting to tire; the stress of the situation accelerated his fatigue.

Jack heard rushing water off in the distance to his right. He looked and saw an enormous wall of water—maybe sixty feet high. It had started far out at sea, but was quickly approaching land. He estimated that they had less than two minutes before it engulfed the coast.

Lucy was easily keeping pace with her father, but while running, she turned to the side to get a look. As she did so, she slipped on some loose rock. It sent her to the ground and rolling downhill a few feet before she stopped herself.

"Lucy!" Jack yelled, running to help her get to her feet.

"I'm fine," she said, seemingly more embarrassed than hurt. They both began to run again.

"Keep running, Peter!" Jack hollered.

Peter reached the summit of the hill and turned the corner, out of Jack's sight. Jack's breathing was rapid and heavy, burning his lungs. He was exhausted. His body was depleted from lack of nutrition. Scurrying through the dense jungle had taken a lot of energy, and now running up a steep hill was draining. It was only by adrenaline that he was able to continue. He looked to his right and saw the massive wave approaching. It was less than a mile from hitting land.

Jack and Lucy finally reached the top of the hill. Jack saw Peter standing just a short way in a cave. He was not moving at all. He seemed to be frozen, his sight fixated on something.

Jack was worried about entering the cave, concerned that water could wash them in to who knows where, but since the opening was angled to the side, it may also provide some protection from the initial force of the wave.

Jack and Lucy ran in about fifteen feet. Peter was still frozen. It was quite dark and had a damp, moldy smell. Then Jack noticed that the wall seemed to be moving. The light from outside was faint this far back in the cave, so Jack pulled his backpack off and removed one of the flashlights, closed the backpack, and threw it around his shoulders. A click of the button provided a stream of light. Jack's eyes grew wide with terror. The wall wasn't moving—it was filled with spiders. Different sizes. Different types. But his eye caught a few tarantulas and Brazilian Wandering Spiders.

Jack scanned other sections of the cave. His fear was confirmed. The spiders were not just on the wall. They seemed to be all over the cave. It was as if they walked into a giant nest of dangerous arachnids. Jack wondered if there were any that were already crawling on his back.

"Oh my goodness," Lucy said softly, seeing the surrounding danger. Her voice was filled with terror but subdued, as if not to disturb the surrounding creatures. "What do we do? What do we do?" she asked, her voice trembling.

Peter was as still as a statue.

"Let's get out of here!" Jack yelled.

Just as they started to move, Jack heard massive rushing water and collapsing trees. It was chilling.

"Run!" he said. He dropped the spear and grabbed each of their shirts, afraid he might lose them when the water hit.

They didn't make it back to the opening before water swooshed into the cave. At first it was only knee high, but it was powerful and stopped their progress toward the opening. But the water quickly rose and started to pull them backward and apart.

Lucy screamed, "Dad!"

"I have you! Hold on to me!"

Jack tried to maintain his ground as Lucy and Peter tried to cling to him, but water level quickly rose to their chest and the force was far too powerful. It knocked them off their feet, sending them against a back wall that separated their grasps. Jack tried to hold on, but the water swirled with tremendous force.

"Lucy! Peter!" he yelled, barely above water. The current swept them farther back, beyond the initial wall that separated them.

Screams filled the cave, echoing off the walls.

Jack swished around in the water, trying to find his kids. His fingers felt the legs of a spider swirling in the water. Another spider grabbed onto his forehead, but Jack quickly smacked it off.

"Lucy! Peter!" he yelled again, this time swallowing a gulp of salty water. Jack was being taken for a ride, farther into the cave, and he had no idea where Lucy and Peter were. It was very dark.

Within seconds Jack hit a wall at the back of the cave. But he didn't stop there. The water carried him down a hole at the back of the cave. He was completely submerged. He instinctively held his breath.

The drop was straight down. There was no way to swim against the powerful force of the rushing water. Jack decided it was better to protect himself rather than fight the gushing water. He held his arms in front of his face to guard his head. The force of the water was incredibly strong, bouncing Jack along the jagged walls. He continued underwater and was losing oxygen quickly.

His lower back smashed against a rock, causing a sharp pain to run down his spine. His arms tried to push away from the wall, but the swirling water swung his body around and his cheek scraped against rock, scratching his skin. He finally pushed away, but continued to descend. Jack wondered how far he was dropping and began to feel that time was running out.

I'm going to drown, he thought to himself, unsure how far down in the earth the water was going to carry him. *There is no way to get back up. I'm going to drown.*

Jack's feet finally hit ground, possibly the bottom of a cave. He was just about out of air. He kicked off the bottom to try to get to the surface. He rose about ten feet and his head broke through the water line. He gasped for air, choking on some water. The saltiness was strong, both the taste and smell.

"Lucy! Peter!" he yelled. It echoed in what seemed to be a large pit. It was very dark. There was no visibility.

There was no response. The sound of rushing water continued to pour in from above. It echoed loudly off the walls. Jack waded in the water, unable to touch the bottom. He frantically swished around, trying to feel for his children. He yelled again for them.

"Dad!" Lucy screamed, between choking on water and gasping for air. It sounded like she had just emerged from underwater and was within arm's reach. Jack extended his arms in the direction of her voice.

"Lucy! Reach out."

Eventually their extended arms found each other. Jack grabbed Lucy's arm and pulled her closer. They were both kicking and wading in the saltwater.

"Are you okay?" Jack asked.

"Yeah," she replied as she coughed out water.

"Peter!" Jack screamed, pleading to find his son.

The sound of rushing water was beginning to dissipate, as if the wave was almost finished invading the cave.

"Where is Peter?" Jack asked.

"I don't know," Lucy whimpered.

Then Jack heard coughing about ten feet away. "Peter!"

"I ... I ..." Peter muttered in between forcing some water out of his lungs. "I'm okay."

"Don't move. We'll come to you," Jack ordered.

Jack nudged Lucy in Peter's direction, and they both started to swim over. The cave remained dark, but they were able to find Peter clinging to a wall.

"Are you hurt?"

"I hit my shoulder but I'm okay," Peter muttered in between taking long, deep breaths.

Jack noticed that the water level was steadily dropping, as if draining deep into the earth.

"Hold onto the wall!" Jack ordered. "The water is getting lower, but I'm not sure where the water is draining. We don't want to get dragged into some hidden crevices."

Jack wiped the salty water away from his face. The salt stung his eyes a little and tasted terrible on his lips. But he was grateful they were alive.

Soon they could touch the floor of the pit with their feet. They heard rushing water beneath them, somewhere in the lower depths of the cave. Fortunately, they started to get a little bit of visibility. A faint amount of daylight penetrated the pit from a small opening, about ten feet away. It had initially been below the water, but as the water level dropped, the opening allowed some light; otherwise the pit would have been pitch black.

Having lost the first flashlight in the flood, Jack removed his backpack from around his shoulders, opened it, and found the other flashlight. He removed it, hoping it would still work. He clicked the button and was relieved to see a small beam of light. He saw Peter holding onto a wall, exasperated and still coughing. Lucy was next to Jack, beginning to shiver from being soaked.

He used the small light to scan the pit. It was smaller than he expected. It seemed to be about fifteen feet from side to side. He looked up, examining where they came from. The drop was about twenty feet through a narrow opening, and the vertical incline was completely smooth, providing no crevices to grab. It would be impossible to climb back up.

The seawater continued to recede through some holes that descended further underground. Jack felt aches on his arms and legs. The adrenaline was wearing off, and the pain was apparent. Nothing seemed too severe—just bumps and bruises.

"How do we get out of here?" Lucy asked.

"I don't know," Jack answered. "I'm not sure we can climb back up." Actually Jack knew that would be almost impossible but didn't want to fully admit that yet.

Suddenly, Jack felt something swoop by his head. He heard flapping wings and ducked out of instinct. He directed the flashlight toward the movement, but didn't see anything.

"What was that?" Peter asked with a bit of dread, as if he wasn't sure he wanted an answer.

"I ... uhh ... I'm not sure," Jack answered. He had an inclination but didn't want to say it before confirming. He flashed the light higher and saw something fly high above; then it landed on a portion of the ceiling not affected by the water, joining several other shadowy figures.

"What is that?" Lucy asked with dread, as if she suspected the answer.

Jack examined the creatures hanging upside down from the ceiling. They had large ears and furry heads. Their long, bony arms held their folded wings in tight, wrapped around their bodies. Other than an occasional rocking, they were generally motionless, hanging from the ceiling in a chilling fashion. It confirmed his initial suspicion.

"Bats," Jack said. "Vampire bats."

"Vampire? Really?" Peter said with a mix of skepticism and trepidation.

"Really," Jack said matter-of-factly.

"Vampire," Lucy said in a faint voice, causing Jack to realize that maybe he shouldn't have included that point.

He knew why they were called that. Their food source was blood. They used their sharp fangs to bite their victims and then literally licked the blood. Obviously no need to mention that.

Jack continued scanning the walls, searching for a way out.

"There must be a dozen of them," Peter said. There was no way to know. The light was no longer on the ceiling, but he was clearly pondering what he had seen.

"I don't want to know," Lucy said, shaking her head. "We have to get out of here."

"No kidding!" Peter replied.

"Quiet!" Jack snapped, afraid they would quickly descend into uncontrollable panic. "I need to think."

The water finished receding. The floor was wet but no longer completely covered in water. Jack scanned the rocky ground. Other than the occasional boulder and a few small slopes, the ground was generally flat. He looked for where the water may have drained and eventually found numerous holes at a low spot against a wall. Nothing large enough to fit through, but certainly big enough for the water to quickly drain.

Jack continued to flash the light around and froze when he saw some small movement on the rocky floor.

"What's that?" Peter asked with fear.

Jack didn't need to respond. The flashlight confirmed it.

Sprinkled around the floor were spiders, including some Brazilian Wandering Spiders. They were shriveled up from the water, but a few of them were moving a bit, starting to awaken.

"What are we gonna do?" Peter pleaded, clearly beginning to descend into a state of panic.

Jack looked back at the small opening with daylight coming through. It looked to be only a little larger than twelve inches. It was up a small slope of rocks and Jack ran up to examine it closer. He could see through the hole that there was flat rock on the other side of the opening.

"We can't fit through there," Lucy declared.

Jack grabbed the edges of the opening and pulled, trying to pry some rocks free, but there was no give at all. He tried another side and a small rock moved slightly, giving him some hope. He yanked with all his strength. It broke free and rolled down the slope. The opening was slightly larger now, about eighteen inches wide. Jack tried to open it wider, but the rest of the rock was unmovable.

"Go through!" Jack yelled.

"We can't fit." Peter said.

"We have to!" Jack exclaimed. "Do you want to stay here with the spiders and bats? Let's go!"

Lucy didn't hesitate. She threw herself into the hole. She wiggled herself through the opening, scraping her arms against the edges, but made it through.

"Go!" Jack ordered Peter.

Peter hesitated.

"Think about the spiders waking up in this dark pit," Jack said, hoping that would provide the nudge of motivation Peter might need. He was a little bigger than Lucy, so it would be more difficult.

Something must have clicked in his mind, perhaps spiders, because he threw himself at the hole. "Ahhhhh!" Peter shouted, as he started to squeeze between the narrow rocks. Jack grabbed his legs and pushed, assisting Peter, who was trying to wiggle through.

Halfway through, Peter said, "Lucy, pull my arm."

Peter continued to struggle, at one point almost becoming frantic. But inch by inch, he progressed through the hole. He finished by yanking his feet away from the opening.

Jack was relieved and concerned—relieved his children made it through, but then wondering how he, easily the largest of the three, was going to fit through the opening.

Jack shoved the backpack through the hole. He thought about removing his shirt but decided against it.

"I'm coming," Jack said. He put his right arm through first and then his head. *There is no way I'm going to fit,* he thought to himself. But he forced himself through as hard as he could. His right shoulder popped clear, but he couldn't get his left shoulder through the opening. He kicked as hard as he could.

"Grab my hand," Jack said.

Lucy and Peter grabbed and started to pull him through. His left shoulder popped through, but he was only able to move forward another six inches or so before his left arm got locked against his body. He was wedged in very tight. They continued to try to pull, but he was not moving anymore.

His torso was stuck. He kicked against the ground to try to force himself through, but he could not get beyond a certain point. He felt the pressure of the rock around his body, making it impossible to take a deep breath.

"I'm stuck," Jack said. Peter and Lucy tried another yank, but there was no movement, only pain.

"Wait! Wait!" Jack said, "Let me catch my breath." He tried to pull backward, but that was even worse. He couldn't get enough footing to pull himself back through, and his left arm was firmly pinned against his body.

Jack began to feel claustrophobic. He was crammed tightly between massive stone that had no give. On top of that, his bare legs hung in a cave that was filled with vampire bats and waking spiders. At some point, something was going to get hungry.

CHAPTER 8

Jack was trying to resist having a panic attack. Being stuck between massive, solid rock was terrifying. He tried to take deep breaths, but the narrow opening where he was wedged was constricting, squeezing his torso. His inhales and exhales were short and fast paced. He could feel his anxiety level rising, wreaking havoc with his body—increasing his heart rate, causing more perspiration, and creating a massive pit in his stomach.

How am I going to get out of here? How will I be able help my kids survive?

He had been stuck for less than an hour, but the feeling of helplessness was overwhelming. To stop himself from hyperventilating, Jack closed his eyes to focus on breathing and try to settle himself. He lowered his head onto his right arm to try to take a break from worrying. Thinking about his children or wife only made him worry more; instead he focused on God. He prayed, asking God to settle his panic and somehow help him break free.

Jack's thoughts were interrupted when he heard footsteps. He popped his eyes open and looked up. Peter came running from the other side of the hill, "Dad. There's a bridge."

"What?"

"It's a rope bridge that extends over a canyon."

"No way," Lucy said. She had been running alongside him. "I'm not crossing that. Looks flimsy. Way, way too high."

Peter continued. "There's no way to climb down this hill. There are sharp drops on every side and we are blocked by a high wall from getting to the slope that we came up. Plus, there looks like a small house on the other side after we cross the bridge."

"How long is the bridge?" Jack asked.

"Long," Lucy said.

"I don't know—maybe thirty feet," Peter answered. "It's over a chasm of rocks. And to the right of those rocks there is a small stream."

"A stream?" Jack asked. "You mean seawater?"

"I don't think so. It's flowing water. It's clearly coming from somewhere else," Peter answered.

Jack raised his eyebrows, wondering if it could provide them some fresh water, if they could get to it.

Suddenly, Jack felt a light touch on his bare leg. Something was starting to crawl onto his flesh. *A spider. No doubt about it. A large one.* He felt each of its eight long legs as it slowly climbed onto his left calf muscle. It was large—probably six inches in diameter. The legs were dangly, like a Brazilian Wandering Spider.

Jack froze, not wanting to startle it. He hoped it would climb off, but it seemed to settle, perhaps enjoying the heat from his flowing blood.

Jack felt a strong desire to kick the spider off, but feared it would cling to his skin and bite before he could shake it free. That said, it could bite anyway, at any moment. He wondered how long he could remain steady. Any vibration may startle or anger the spider.

"Lucy. Peter," Jack said in a low voice. "A spider has climbed onto my leg." Jack exhaled slowly. "It's not leaving."

"Oh my goodness," Peter said, his bulging eyes revealing his fear.

"What can we do?" Lucy asked.

"If something happens to me. If I don't make it …"

"Stop," Lucy said. "I don't want to hear that."

Suddenly, the spider began to sink its fangs into Jack's leg. The pain was excruciating. It felt as if someone took a sharp nail, placed it on his left calf muscle, and banged the head with a hammer. Jack smacked the spider away with his right leg.

"I'm bit!" Jack shouted. "I'm bit!"

Jack reached his right hand up to Lucy and Peter. They both grabbed his arm and began to yank as hard as possible.

"Pull hard! Don't stop!" Jack yelled. He worried the angry spider was preparing for an attack somewhere else on his legs. Or maybe it would climb under his shirt and bite his back. Other flashes of dread filled his mind. If there was any blood, it would attract the vampire bats. He may become a human feeding bag for all the creatures lurking in the cave.

Lucy and Peter continued to pull with all their might. Jack exhaled every ounce of air he could in order to try to shrink his torso. At first no movement; but then he edged forward half of an inch. With the surrounding rock compressed against his body, he could no longer take breaths. Within moments he was already running out of air.

Then Jack moved forward an inch. The top rock that was pressed against his back began to tear his clothes and scrape his back. He didn't feel too much pain yet. The adrenaline coursing through his body was dulling the sting of his skin being deeply scratched.

Suddenly there was a pop. Jack's right shoulder had dislocated from the pulling. The adrenaline was not enough to subdue that pain. He yelled, "Ahhhh!"

Before he could yell "Stop," his left arm and torso that had been firmly wedged, squeezed through the opening. The rest of his body slid through easily. Lucy and Peter pulled Jack away from the hole.

Jack was lying on the ground but felt as though he may lose consciousness from the agonizing pain. He gathered enough energy to lift his head and speak. "Cover the hole. Cover it before anything gets out."

With one eye propped open, Jack watched them run around, frantically gathering rocks and branches. It was fairly sparse on the hill, but Lucy and Peter found enough natural objects to cover the hole. Apparently not completely satisfied, Peter dug some dirt with his bare hands and added it to the pile, packing it in.

Jack took large, deep breaths to fill his lungs. "Help me up," he said in a weak voice.

Lucy and Peter helped him to his feet, but Jack didn't want to put a lot of pressure on his left leg. He felt a burning sensation on the spot of the bite and wondered how much danger he was in. If it was a Brazilian Wandering Spider, he knew they were among the most venomous spiders in the world and untreated bites can lead to death. *The bite was quick, so maybe any venom injected would be minimal,* he thought. He hoped.

Jack hopped over to one of the few trees on the small hill. He grabbed it firmly with his left hand. "My shoulder is out of socket." Large drops of sweat were popping out of Jack's forehead, and he felt nausea.

Lucy and Peter stood without speaking, clearly unsure of what to do.

Knowing Lucy could not handle what was to come next, Jack looked at Peter "I need you …" Jack took a breath and fought back the inclination to vomit. "I need you to hit my shoulder. Knock it back into place."

Peter hesitated; then slowly raised his arms and placed his hands together, forming a human ramming rod. Peter hesitated again. "I … what do you want me to do?"

"Ram your hands into my shoulder." Jack pointed to the front of his right shoulder with his left index finger. "Right here," he said. Jack dropped his head. The pain sapping the energy from his body made it difficult to stand.

Peter hesitated, "I don't know. I …"

"Do it!" Jack ordered.

Peter clasped both hands together tightly and rammed them into his dad's shoulder.

"Ahhhhh!" Jack yelled. He felt a pop back in place, as if it worked, but it was accompanied by a jolt of pain that exploded in his shoulder. He stumbled and then collapsed to his knees.

Peter stepped back without a word.

"It worked," Jack said with some level of relief. "Back in place."

Jack felt more nausea and chills. He told himself he needed to be mentally tough and push forward. Again he fought back the inclination to vomit. That would certainly make him more dehydrated. He pulled himself back to his feet to get a look around.

A large wall was behind them leading to the higher portion of the hill. There was no way around the wall, and it was vertical and smooth, making climbing up it impossible. There would be no way to get back to the front where they had run up. They were nestled on a lower level but still high up, at least thirty feet. Below were jagged rocks protruding from the remnants of the tsunami.

Much of the coast was swamped with ocean water. *A bad sign for getting drinking water or dry wood for a fire*, he thought. The tsunami invaded the coast quite far ahead, beyond their site. A few large hills inland and a smattering of tall trees stood out.

"The bridge is this way." Peter pointed. He headed toward the back of the small hill, which was about twenty feet in diameter.

Jack limped along to get a look.

"There's the bridge," Peter said, pointing at it with his right index finger. "And there's the house." He raised his finger slightly to show the location.

Jack's eyes went right to the house. He wanted to start with some positive news. On the other side of the chasm, about a quarter mile after the bridge, a small house sat on top of another large hill.

"We haven't seen anyone," Lucy said. "Is it someone's house?"

"I don't know," Jack answered as he reached for the backpack Lucy was now holding. With his right hand, he gingerly pulled out the small pair of binoculars. His right shoulder still throbbed with pain. He transferred the binoculars to his left hand and brought them to his eyes to examine the structure.

It was a small, square-shaped house, built with logs. What

appeared to be the front door faced the ocean. Two large windows were on either side of the door; no broken glass. A chimney extended above the roof on the left side of the house, indicating it had a fireplace. Overall, the structure looked worn but functional. A few trees were scattered around it, but otherwise it was in a fairly open area. There was no sign of movement, or any recent activity.

"Looks more like some kind of cabin, instead of someone's home. There's obviously no electricity or running water. But it looks promising. It will protect us from the weather, and I bet there are some supplies in there."

Jack lowered the binoculars and examined the bridge. There were three main, heavy-duty ropes forming the base of the structure. Two on each side for the railings and one on the bottom, forming a V. Smaller ropes connected the railings to the bottom rope. Weather had clearly taken a toll on the rope, which was frayed in some areas, no doubt the impact from rain and strong winds from the ocean.

Jack paused, feeling more chills. He dropped his head slightly but then forced himself to look again at the house. *It definitely looks promising*, he thought.

Jack's vision became a little blurry. He squinted to try to focus his eyesight, but the blurriness continued to get worse. Jack saw three houses now instead of one. The ground was getting fuzzy. Trees looked like they were floating above the ground.

"Need to lie down," Jack said in a weak voice. He dropped to his right knee to ensure he didn't fully collapse. He allowed himself to gently settle to the ground and lie down. *Venom must be kicking in*, Jack thought.

Jack felt his body temperature rising; he began to tremble from chills. He didn't want his kids to see him in this condition, but there was no way to control the shivering. Vomit came up to the back of his throat, but Jack kept his mouth closed and swallowed the stomach bile. The whole world seemed to be spinning, so Jack decided to close his eyes.

"Dad!" Lucy said, her tone filled with panic. "Are you okay?"

"I feel … weak." The bite on his calf was burning, while the rest of his body continued to shake with chills. "I just need to rest."

"Do you want me to cross the bridge and go to the house?" Peter asked. "See if there is anyone who can help?"

"No!" Jack answered. "Not yet. I don't want you to cross without me." Jack placed his left hand on his forehead and felt a thick coat of sweat. "But if something happens to me …"

"Stop!" Lucy said. "You're going to be fine. Think positive. We need you."

"I need to rest," Jack muttered. "I don't know how long."

"It's still early in the day," Peter said. "But even when the sun goes down later, I think we'll be fine. We don't have a fire, but I think we're pretty safe up here."

Unless the spiders get out, Jack thought to himself. He didn't have the energy to turn and check the barricade they had made.

Jack took deep breaths. Then he stopped taking deep breaths and just lay motionless.

"Ahh … let's talk about something, Dad," Lucy said. "You're making me really nervous."

"Sure," Jack said softly. He no longer felt the need to vomit and the chills were manageable. He was fairly content lying down with his eyes closed, comfortable enough to talk.

"Umm … what would be most interesting?"

Jack didn't answer. He felt light–headed. Dizzy.

"Umm …" Lucy started. "It may surprise you, but I have been thinking about what you said about Jesus. You know—that He claimed to be God."

The topic grabbed Jack's attention. He listened intently.

Lucy continued, "Aren't there are a lot of religious leaders who claimed to be God? Why is Jesus different?"

"Well," Jack said, happy to get his mind off the pain. "Actually there aren't a lot of religious founders who claimed to be God. Not any of the major religions. Jesus is unique in that way."

"But just because He said it, that doesn't make it true, right?"

she countered. "Why do you believe He is God?" Her tone was inquisitive, not the usual hostility and sarcasm.

"Jesus did miracles, proving His claims, validating His identity," Jack said softly. "He even referred to them as evidence if His disciples could not simply accept His claim to be God.[84] In other words, Jesus was open to evidence confirming His identity."

"Evidence … hmmm," Peter muttered.

"I get it," Lucy said. "But to be honest, Dad, it's hard to believe the miracles of the Bible. I mean walking on water?[85] Healing diseases?[86] Feeding at least five thousand people from a couple of loaves of bread?"[87] Lucy frowned. "How can you just believe they are true?"

A new wave of symptoms came over Jack. The world seemed to be spinning. He felt a fever on the inside and a chill on the outside against his sweaty skin. But to him this discussion was just too important. He forced himself to stay focused.

"Well." Jack paused to rub his forehead. "As we discussed before, there are good reasons to believe the Bible is historically reliable and true and that God inspired the authors. You remember, right? Thousands of manuscripts. Embarrassing details. Prophecies. Et cetera. We didn't even discuss the archaeology that also supports the Bible. Based on these reasons, I believe the accounts that are recorded in the Bible are true."

Not hearing an immediate response, Jack decided to continue. "Plus, miracles are not hard to believe. I mean, the beginning of the universe is a well-evidenced event, and something coming from nothing is quite the miracle. If you believe that, which has good evidence, and that God exists, which also has good evidence, then the possibility of other miracles in the Bible is quite easy to accept."[88]

"I guess so," Lucy conceded. "But why don't we see miracles today?"

"Oh, I believe miracles are definitely happening today," Jack answered. "We have cases of miraculous healings in modern times,[89] but some in the medical profession call them spontaneous healings instead of miracles."

The discussion about miraculous healings reminded him of his current condition. He felt his body battling the poison. The icy chills continued to shake his body. His heart was rapid, thumping heavily in his chest. He paused a moment to pray in his mind for his health.

Dear God, thank You for watching over us through all these dangers. Thank You for helping me escape from being stuck between the rocks. If it is within Your will, please heal me of this poison. Please continue to watch over us. In Jesus's name. Amen.

"What about miracles in the Bible?" Lucy asked. "Even if they are possible, why believe they actually happened?"

"Sometimes there are embarrassing details included in the miracle accounts. Since it is highly unlikely the author would have included embarrassing details if he were fabricating the story, it provides good reason to believe the miracles occurred."

"That's actually pretty interesting." Lucy admitted. "What's an example?"

Jack took a big, deep breath. "When Jesus healed a demon possessed man, He allowed the evil spirits to enter pigs that ran into the sea. Skeptics may scoff at that account, but consider the embarrassing manner in which the account ends. The townspeople were made aware of this event, and when they came out to Jesus, they did not praise Him for the miracle. Rather, they asked Him to leave their region.[90] That's an embarrassing reaction to an extraordinary healing. If the story were made up, it likely would have ended much differently, probably with the people of the town glorifying and worshiping Jesus, not asking Him to leave. That subtle detail is one good reason to believe that the event is true."

Jack continued. "The most important miracle, though, is Jesus's resurrection. There are good historical reasons to believe the resurrection happened."

"I thought the resurrection was something you believe in spite of the evidence," Lucy said. "Like blind faith."

"No!" Jack said, speaking loudly. "Although you don't need historical facts to believe in Jesus, they do support His resurrection. You don't need to trust in Jesus based on blind faith."

"Facts? What historical facts?" Lucy asked.

"The majority of scholars who study the historical evidence on this topic believe there are a few core facts. I'm talking about scholars who are Christians and non-Christians."

"What are the facts?" Lucy pushed.

"Number one, Jesus died by crucifixion. Number two, His disciples had experiences that they truly believed were with the risen Jesus. Number three, Paul, who was initially an enemy of Christians, claimed to have experienced the risen Jesus and became a believer. Number four, James, who was Jesus's brother and initially a skeptic before Jesus's crucifixion, became a believer after the resurrection. Number five, the tomb Jesus was buried in was found empty."[91]

"Really?" Lucy said in a surprised tone. "These are considered facts by historical scholars?"

"Absolutely," Jack affirmed. "Regarding evidence for the resurrection, think of the acronym ACE, which stands for appearances to the disciples, conversions of Paul and James, and the empty tomb. They are well evidenced from an historical perspective."

"If they are considered facts, why aren't all these scholars Christians?" Peter asked.

"Sometimes people choose to believe what they want, in spite of the evidence. Those who don't believe Jesus was resurrected will argue that something else happened, something other than a supernatural miracle. They may not know what, but they rule out a miracle as even possible. The problem for them is that there is no natural explanation that fits all of this evidence."

Lucy frowned, "Really? I mean … Honestly, there are so many other things that could have happened instead of a real resurrection."

"Like what?" Jack asked.

"Maybe Jesus didn't really die," Lucy said. "What is more likely?

The Romans who executed Him made a mistake or Jesus rose from the dead?"

"Jesus rose from the dead," Jack answered in a matter-of-fact manner. "Most people who were crucified died from either shock or asphyxiation.[92]"

"Asphyxiation? What's that?" Peter asked.

Hearing the word *asphyxiation* made Jack wonder if his throat might swell and close up from the venom, blocking his air passage. He took a deep breath to make sure that wasn't beginning to happen.

"When someone hangs from a crucifixion, they cannot exhale," Jack answered. "The person needs to pull up to breathe. But this is painful and tiring. When the person is no longer able to pull up, they suffocate to death. Consequently, there is no way to fake death by hanging for a long period of time. Same goes for Jesus—He would not have been able to hang for a long period of time and fake His death."

"That's why Romans sometimes broke the legs of people being crucified. To speed up the process." Lucy admitted. Her demeanor was clearly friendly. Either her goal was to keep her father talking because she was concerned or she was genuinely interested in learning. Maybe both.

"That's exactly right, Lucy. Also, the Romans sometimes delivered a fatal blow to ensure the victim was dead. In Jesus's case, they stabbed His heart. The Bible records water and blood coming from Jesus's side; the reference to water is quite possibly the sac of water that is next to the heart."[93]

"Yeah, I remember reading that somewhere in the Bible," Lucy admitted.

"Also, if Jesus did not die on the cross, we can't reconcile this with the experiences the disciples had, nor the appearance to and conversion of Paul."[94]

"What do you mean?" Lucy asked. "If Jesus didn't die and then His disciples saw Him alive, they might have thought He just rose from the dead."

"Highly unlikely." Jack quickly countered, "If Jesus had appeared to the disciples in a ravaged condition, they would not have thought He rose from the dead. Rather, they would probably have tried to get Him a doctor."[95]

"Well . . ." Lucy said. She paused, as if trying to think of something else. "What about hallucinations? I've heard some people say that maybe the disciples had experiences, but they were hallucinations. Visions. Not the real Jesus."

"I appreciate you are really thinking about this," Jack said tenderly. "But again, that doesn't work. First, people don't have group hallucinations.[96] Yes, individual people have hallucinations, but they don't have the same hallucination with other people around them. In the Bible, some of the recorded appearances were to multiple people at the same time; this includes one instance when Jesus appeared to over five hundred at one time, which was recorded in a very early creed dated within two to eight years from the resurrection."[97]

Jack rubbed the temples on his forehead to soothe his dizziness. Fortunately the chills seemed to be subsiding.

"Also, Paul, who was previously an enemy of Christians, was not in the frame of mind to have a vision. And don't forget the empty tomb—a hallucination clearly does not fit with that piece of evidence. Finally, there are accounts of Jesus breaking bread and eating with the disciples[98] as well as offering His disciple Thomas the opportunity to touch Him to convince him He was risen.[99] That's hardly possible with an hallucination."

"Maybe the disciples just lied," Lucy said, clearly trying another option.

"Again, not likely," Jack said. "Why would they make this claim and be willing to die for it?[100] Some people are willing to die for a cause, but not if they clearly know it is a lie.[101] Also, James, Jesus's brother, was a skeptic before seeing the resurrected Jesus and would not have been in on this plot. Finally, think about Paul.[102] He was an enemy of Christians before experiencing the risen Jesus. He definitely wouldn't have been in on this scheme. Remember, Paul had an entirely different experience.[103] What led to his conversion if not for a true experience with the Lord?"

"Well there must be some explanation," Lucy stated.

"Yes. Jesus rose from the dead," Jack stated plainly. "It is the best explanation of the historical facts. And ... if you believe that God exists, which we have already discussed good reasons to believe that—the beginning of the universe, design in the universe, morality—then believing in the resurrection is not that difficult to accept."

"But what if you're wrong, Dad?" Lucy asked in a pleasant tone.

Jack propped himself up on his elbows and faced his children. Lucy's eyes widened, as if surprised her Dad was able to do that.

"What if you're wrong?" Jack countered with a kind tone. He waited a moment to let that question sink in. "If I'm wrong, well I think I've lived a good life anyway. A great life, actually. And if atheism is true then I will simply cease to exist, never knowing the difference. Or if something else is true and I'm reincarnated, I'll have another chance at getting things right."

Jack's face became more intense. "But if Christianity is true, then this is *our one chance.* We have one life to get our eternal destination right. I would rather put my trust in Jesus to save my soul from the punishment I deserve for my sins, rather than turn my back on my Creator and live whatever short life I wanted, which ultimately leads to eternal separation from God. We all have to decide, and our preferences for what we hope is true are irrelevant. I think all the evidence for Christianity makes it a fairly easy decision."

"I ... I don't know, Dad. I need to think about it," Lucy admitted.

Jack lowered himself back to a prone position. He was actually beginning to feel a little better and quite drowsy. "I'm glad you're a critical thinker. You probably get that from me. But I was naïve in just assuming you would believe in God and follow Jesus. When you were little, I used to worry about your physical well-being—that you would grow up healthy and safe. But now? My biggest fear is *what you decide about God.*"

"After everything we have been through? That's your biggest fear?" Lucy asked with a bit of shock.

"Is there anything more important than eternity?" Jack countered. "Of course there are things I worry about here on Earth. I'm human, after all. I'm your father and want to protect you. But I'm trying to get you home. Not just home to Mom but also to your spiritual home—heaven. It is my biggest fear for both of you."

"Me?" Peter asked with a bit of shock. "I'm a Christian."

"I hope so," Jack said with tenderness.

Jack noticed that Peter's facial expression was surprised— somewhat stunned actually.

"What do you mean?" Peter asked, clearly insulted at the question. "I go to church with you."

"There is an *eternal* difference between being a Christian, a true follower of Jesus, versus going through the motions," Jack said. "I definitely don't want to insult you, Peter. Really. But honestly, I'm worried. I don't know if you truly believe and are committed to Christ. In some ways, I'm more worried about you than Lucy."

"Really?" Lucy and Peter said simultaneously.

"Someone who claims to be a Christian but isn't really a follower of Jesus may have a false sense of security. They think they are all set, but actually they are in danger of hell. To me, one of the scariest verses in the Bible is when Jesus said that there would be those who claim to be Christians and He will say, 'Away from me, I never knew you.'[104] I don't ever want that to be you, Peter. I pray that you are truly committed to the Lord Jesus, and I am here to help you in any way I can. I love you both."

"Hmmm." Peter grunted. It was different from his typical muttering. No humor. This time it was more reflective. Maybe concerned.

"That's the first time I've heard you admit that you have fear," Lucy said.

"When it comes to fear, I try to live by a simple principle," Jack said. "My one fear is to fear the One."

"What?" Peter asked.

"My one fear is to fear the One," Jack repeated.

"What does it mean?" Lucy asked.

"When Jesus warned His disciples about upcoming persecution, He told them not to fear the one who can kill the body, but rather to fear the One who is able to destroy both body and soul.[105] In other words, fear God. Fear the One who determines the eternal destination of your soul."

Jack motioned with his hand. "Don't get me wrong. I'm human and still have everyday worries, and I don't dismiss real concerns and anxieties that people have. But I constantly remind myself that ultimately all the fears and worries of life pale in comparison to facing eternal punishment. To me, there really is only one fear—God's judgment."

Jack let out a yawn. His body was more relaxed now and he was definitely feeling more tired than sick. Actually very tired. "Did I answer your questions, Lucy?"

"Yeah," she responded. "Kind of rattled my perspective on things."

"That's good," Jack said, satisfied with the discussion. "Let's get some rest. Tomorrow we go to the bridge and cross."

CHAPTER 9

The morning sun slowly pushed away the darkness. It was dawn. Jack was the first to crack open his eyelids. He snapped himself to attention, raising his head to look around.

At first, he was startled by the unfamiliar location; then he remembered how they arrived. The tsunami. The cave. The spiders. He reached down, underneath his leg. There was a large bump. It was warm to the touch, but not too painful. Overall his body felt okay. *The fever seems to have subsided—thank God.*

After a few quick stretches, Jack got himself to his feet. Although the effects of the venom were gone, his body was quite sore. He had multiple bruises from being bounced around in the cave by the flood, and sleeping on rock all night didn't help. He took a moment to look around. The pink sky lit up the coast. *It is a beautiful morning*, he decided. *Sure, the coast is a mess, but we're alive. Why not focus on the positive?*

Jack stepped away quietly, trying not to wake anyone just yet. He noticed that the sounds of the jungle were missing. Most of the birds and other animals were gone. The silence was eerie.

Jack made his way over to the bridge. He examined it closely, looking for potential signs of weakness. His eyes followed the rope across the chasm, looking for any fraying.

I don't see any obvious concerns.

Jack looked over the edge, down toward the bottom. As soon as he did, he wished he hadn't. He was not fond of heights, and it looked about thirty feet down to a bunch of jagged rocks. Clearly the tsunami had swept over the rocks and then rolled away, leaving the sharp, protruding rocks exposed. The small stream that Peter had mentioned was to the right of the rocks, toward the mainland. Jack felt his knees get weak with nervousness. He felt even more vulnerable when a strong breeze came by. He watched the rope bridge sway in the wind—not a significant amount, but enough to be concerning.

Jack exhaled, not realizing he had stopped breathing for a moment. He studied the rope, wondering how the three of them would proceed. He wanted to cross with his kids, stay together just in case. But it clearly did not look strong enough to support all three of them at once. He wondered if it would be strong enough to hold his weight.

His thoughts faded as he heard the crunching of rocks and sand from behind—footsteps that signaled someone was approaching. Lucy stepped up next to her father and gazed at the bridge. "Are we really going to try to cross that? Doesn't look safe to me."

"Good morning, my little girl." Jack shared some of her concerns but knew it was far more dangerous to stay on the hill with no shelter, food, or water. "Unfortunately, there are no other options," Jack said with empathy. "The only way to freedom is to cross. Unless you want to open the hole and enter the pit with spiders and bats," he joked, trying to lighten the mood and trigger a smile from his daughter.

"I'mmm not sure ..." she muttered. Her words tailed off as if her mind was consumed with dreadful thoughts. "Are we going to stay close to each other while we cross?"

"I think we need to go one at a time."

"What? No way."

Jack placed his hand on her shoulder. "It's safer that way. I think it's just strong enough to hold my weight. Any more and it would be too much weight."

Jack heard the crunch of more rocks from behind and turned

to see Peter staggering over, still trying to wake up. He joined them and took a big stretch. "I'm hungry. Let's cross."

Lucy looked over the edge. "Whoa," was all she said.

"Probably better not to look," Jack said.

"I … I can't." Lucy quivered. "I really can't. It's way too high."

It took thirty minutes of discussion, but Lucy finally agreed to go on one condition—she went last. Jack was okay with that. He wanted to go first to test it out. He told her if she didn't come across, then he was going to come back for her.

Jack grabbed the side railings with either hand. He clenched it tightly, as if his life depended on it—literally. He took the first step, placing his right foot sideways across the lower rope so it would not slip off. He paused, taking a moment to reassure himself everything was still okay. He stepped out from the safety of land with his left foot and was now fully on the bridge.

The reality of the situation hit Jack—he was putting his life on the line with this bridge, believing it would keep him safe. A quick glance at the bottom reminded him how high up he was. He prayed to himself as he slowly proceeded.

Initially, the bridge was more wobbly than expected. But as he completed another couple of steps, it stretched until it reached a point of tension and the vibrations lessened.

"No problem," Jack said out loud, trying to sound convincing to Lucy and Peter, although he continued to feel nervous, being so high up.

The possibility of the rope snapping popped into Jack's mind. His hands began to perspire. He forced the thought out of his mind. *Stay positive. Keep moving.*

He continued to put one foot in front of the other, being very careful to stay balanced. His pace was slow and steady. The occasional wobble wreaked havoc with his nerves. Butterflies swarmed in his stomach. His hands were slick with sweat, which worried him all the more.

Don't look down, he told himself. Need to set an example. Stay calm.

The middle was the worst. His weight caused the bridge to really stretch and sag. He tightened his grip, just in case the rope snapped. He was greatly concerned that the rope could not hold his weight and glad he insisted that they each go one at a time.

Questions began to pop into his mind. *Who built this bridge? Did they know what they were doing? How long has it been here? How many times has rain soaked its fibers? Did the tsunami weaken it to a point of breaking? Why didn't I ask myself these questions before I started?*

The questions were rapid. They continued to pepper his mind, viciously attacking his nerves. Jack shook the thoughts away and resumed his progress, pulling himself along. Getting past the halfway point was reassuring. His confidence grew with each step. Momentum built, and he made good progress.

As he approached the far end, he noticed the ropes were far more tattered and worn on this end. He reached out and felt the fibers that were frayed. It was definitely concerning, but he reassured himself that it apparently held together enough for him to make it across.

Jack stepped off the bridge and onto the ledge. He let out a big breath while facing away from his kids and then turned around toward them. He cupped his hands around his mouth and yelled across the chasm, "All right, Peter. Your turn. Slow and steady. Be careful!"

Jack watched as Peter carefully stepped onto the bridge. Ignoring his father's guidance, he looked down at the rocks below. Jack wondered if that might halt his progress, and initially Peter did pause. But then he took a small step. Then another. Peter seemed to gain confidence with each move forward, and his pace increased.

"Great job, Peter!" Jack hollered. He felt good about the progress Peter was making but then worried he might get overconfident, perhaps go a little too fast and get sloppy with a step. "Stay focused,"

Jack yelled. "Good pace. Don't go too fast. Slow and steady. You got this."

Peter looked forward, apparently checking how far he was from the end. He took another step, but it slipped by the bottom rope and he stumbled. His arms clung to the railings as his foot dangled in midair. He froze, his face filled with terror.

Jack's heart sank when Peter slipped. He wanted to jump out to grab Peter, but he was still well out of reach. Jack let out a breath, releasing the jolt of tension that gripped his nerves when Peter slipped.

After a moment of settling himself, Peter regained his footing and proceeded with caution. A few more careful steps and he made it to the end.

Jack reached his hand out and pulled Peter onto firm ground. He gave his son a tight hug and then a slap on the head, as if to say, "Good job."

Jack turned to Lucy, cupped his hands over his mouth, and again hollered across the chasm. "Okay, your turn. Don't be nervous. Slow and steady."

Jack watched as Lucy put her hands on the rope railings, but hesitated from taking a step. After a few moments, she placed her left foot on the bottom rope, but when the rope wobbled, she stepped back.

Jack refrained from yelling across the chasm and pushing her. *She has to do it without being forced.*

Eventually Lucy got up the nerve to step back onto the bridge. Jack watched as the rope gained tension. It wobbled a bit, perhaps partially from Lucy shaking.

But Lucy took a second step and started to slowly proceed.

"Don't look down at the bottom, Lucy. Just keep focusing on your steps," Jack hollered. "You're doing great."

The bridge seemed to shake most with Lucy. Jack wondered if it was because she weighed the least. He was surprised by how courageous she was. He thought she might not do it and he would need to go back and encourage her to proceed. He was proud of how well she was doing.

As Lucy approached the middle of the bridge, a strong breeze came in from the ocean. The bridge swayed, and Lucy froze. The look on her face was sheer terror.

"Dad!" she cried out.

"It's okay," Jack hollered back. "It'll pass. Just stay still. Stay calm."

Lucy looked over the railing, down toward the bottom.

That's not gonna help, Jack thought.

Lucy's head snapped back up, apparently not thrilled with what she saw.

Eventually, the breeze died down. The swaying of the bridge slowed and then settled.

The tension on Lucy's face eased a bit. She took a small step. And then another. Jack's nerves relaxed slightly with her every step toward him. Eventually she neared the edge.

As Lucy approached the end, Jack was preparing to reach out for her. But suddenly the right railing snapped. It was the section that was frayed the most that gave out. The whole right side of the bridge collapsed. Lucy let out a terrifying scream as she began to fall. Her left hand did not have the strength to hold her entire body weight. Her right hand frantically grabbed the bottom rope for a second, halting her momentum.

Jack lunged at Lucy to grab her, but it was too late. Lucy could not hold on. She fell before Jack could get to her.

"Noooo!" Jack yelled. His emotions exploded inside. Shock and terror filled his mind. He leaned over the edge, dreading the confirmation that his little girl was gone.

He was stunned and relieved to see Lucy. She had fallen onto a small ledge just ten feet below. One foot dangled over the edge, while the rest of her body hugged the safety of the small ledge.

"Lucy!" Jack cried out. "Are you okay?"

She was motionless. At first Jack thought she was unconscious, but then she spoke.

"Dad!" she cried out. "This isn't stable. It's cracking."

Again Jack was filled with panic. There was no way to reach her; he was at a loss of what to do.

Jack watched as Lucy slowly rose to her feet, trying not to make any sudden movements. "Be careful!" he said with panic.

She pressed her hands against the wall of rock and then hugged her body close to the wall. Lucy reached up for Jack's outstretched hand, but they were over a foot apart.

"Peter. Grab a sturdy branch so I can lower it," Jack ordered. "Hurry!"

Without hesitation, Peter ran to find something.

Jack heard rocks crackling from the ledge Lucy was standing on. Then a much louder crackling.

"It's breaking!" Lucy screamed.

Jack couldn't wait for Peter. He swung his legs over the edge and dropped himself as gently as he could to the bottom. Without saying a word, he picked Lucy up and launched her up to the top ledge. The ground cracked loudly as the rocks clearly couldn't hold both their weight. The entire ledge gave out just as Jack boosted Lucy to safety.

Jack felt the ground fall out from under him. His instinct was to grab Lucy's legs and hold on, but he knew that doing so would drag them both to their doom. He refrained and allowed himself to fall.

Time seemed to slow down. As he started to fall, he focused on his daughter. Her body hung over the ledge and grew smaller as he descended. He felt a peace for himself but hoped Lucy and Peter would make it home.

CHAPTER 10

Lucy didn't realize what had happened. The fear of falling and frantic action had caused her to become disoriented. Peter came running to the commotion. He grabbed Lucy's arms and pulled her up and over the edge. Lucy rolled over and watched Peter through her state of fogginess. He leaned over the ledge, looked down below, and yelled, "Daaaaaaad!"

The scream from Peter was like nothing Lucy had ever heard. It quickly tailed off into convulsing tears. Peter dropped his head to the ground, his body shaking with grief.

Peter's actions snapped Lucy out of her daze. Her eyes bulged in terror as she realized what must have happened. She pulled herself to the edge and looked over. Her dad wasn't there. Neither was the ledge. It confirmed her fear—her father was gone. She didn't dare look down at the bottom. For a moment she went numb. Then reality sank in; an avalanche of painful emotions hit her.

Lucy's emotions were overwhelming. For some reason they triggered a memory of her as a little girl. She was maybe six years old and Dad was teaching her to ride a bike. He encouraged her and followed her. She pedaled several feet beyond him, thinking she didn't need him anymore. Then the handlebars wobbled and she fell. Dad was there in an instant to pick her up. She remembered him holding her in his arms. Rocking her. Comforting her. He had always been there. But from now on, he wouldn't.

The memory faded and Lucy was sucked back to reality.

"Nooooooo!" She screamed until her throat hurt. Tears spilled onto the ground. The emotional pain was devastating. Lucy felt shock. Weakness. Then she went unconscious.

United States—about Fifteen Years Later

"So that's how Grandpa died," Zach said softly. His voice was filled with pride instead of sadness.

Lucy closed her eyes and nodded slowly. Her inner eyelids filled with fluid as she fought to keep her emotions under control. She was sitting on the side of Zach's bed as he sat under the covers, with a photograph in hand.

Lucy wiped her right eye just as it was beginning to release a tear. She sniffled away her emotions and looked back at her eight-year-old son. His wide brown eyes watched her closely. His eye color matched his thick brown hair. His mouth was open slightly, as if he had wanted to say something, but he had paused just before the words came out. Lucy offered a loving smile, as if to say everything was okay.

Zach looked down at the picture again that had started the whole conversation. He said he had found it while rummaging through boxes looking for something interesting. He had seen pictures of Grandpa before, but this one was different. It included his mother and Uncle Peter, as well as several strangers from a foreign country, but no Grandma or other family members. It intrigued Zach. He had kept it with him throughout the day, and when Lucy had come in to kiss Zach goodnight, she found him looking at it.

"How did Grandpa die?" was the question Zach had asked almost twenty minutes ago. Immediately Lucy was choked up when Zach showed her the picture. She thought about trying to deflect the question but then decided it was time to tell him the story of how brave his grandpa had been.

The whole story seemed amazing to Zach. Lucy could see that he was brimming with pride at the grandfather he had never met. It also provided a little more background about the world today, which had not yet recovered from the second wave of the deadly disease—D6. The global infrastructure was still decimated. Countries were fractured into numerous segments, and they all struggled to maintain law and order. Communities throughout the planet remained places of fear and isolation. The world was in chaos. Divided. Desperate.

Lucy was determined to change that in the small, rural community where she and Zach now lived. There was danger, no doubt. She had lost her husband five years ago. Zach was young, so he didn't remember his father. It was a difficult environment. But Lucy was now a leader, an inspiration to many, and she routinely gave credit to her Dad.

"He saved me," Lucy said softly, looking at Zach with kind eyes and gently touching his head. "In more ways than one. Not just physically, but spiritually." She looked down, recalling her previous mindset some fifteen years ago. "If it wasn't for Grandpa, I wouldn't be a Christian today. He loved me, took care of me, and shared evidence for Christianity. It changed my thinking. It changed life. It changed my destiny."

"And he saved you from falling," Zach stated, clearly impressed by his grandfather's heroic action.

Lucy smiled. "Yes. It was incredibly selfless for him to jump down to save me."

"Kind of like Jesus coming down and sacrificing Himself to save us," Zach said in a matter-of-fact manner, appropriate for an eight-year-old.

Lucy crumpled her eyebrows with a puzzled look. "Never thought of it that way, but I suppose that's a good way of looking at it." She paused, letting Zach's comment resonate. It was rather common for him to have a unique and interesting perspective on things.

Lucy rubbed his left shoulder, "True love is willing to lay down one's life.[106] Jesus's sacrifice demonstrates God's love for us. It also provides a path to heaven. Some day you will need to decide whether you accept God's gift of salvation, becoming a follower of Jesus."

Zach blinked his big brown eyes and then looked again at the photograph. It was the last picture taken of Grandpa.

"How do you know Grandpa is in heaven?" Zach asked softly.

"We have faith," Lucy answered tenderly. "We trust in Jesus. We believe the Bible gives us the truth about heaven."

"But no one has ever come back after they died. You know … so that we can be sure." Zach was a thinker, like his mother and grandfather.

Lucy gave Zach a puzzled look and smirk. "That's not true. Jesus came back. He was resurrected. He proved He is God and the way to heaven."

"Yes, but that was so long ago. Wouldn't it be great if someone else came back and also told us that there really is life after death?"

Lucy smiled. "Well, actually, there have been many, many people who have died for a short time and been resuscitated back to life, and they have described life after death."

"Really?" Zach's eyes widened, and his mouth fell open. His expression was that of surprise and excitement.

"Yes." Lucy nodded. "These are real events that are called near-death experiences, NDEs for short. Thousands of people have given testimony to life after death. We are careful not to take our beliefs about God from these experiences.[107] Jesus proved He is Lord, so we always follow what He says about heaven. We look to the truth from the Bible. But NDEs provide more confirmation that there is life after death."

"Hmmm," Zach muttered.

Lucy could tell his mind was processing what he had just heard. She had never told him about NDEs before, and it seemed to resonate with him.

"But maybe they're lying," Zach countered. "You know, for attention. How do we know they told the truth?"

"One reason to believe their testimonies are true is that thousands of people have given similar descriptions of what happened.[108] That would be unlikely if they were all lying. Also, children have given similar testimonies as well as people who were born blind."[109]

Lucy watched for Zach's reaction. His face was intense. Focused. He was taking it all in.

She continued. "But I think the biggest reason NDEs are true is that some of the testimonies gave accurate information about something far away from their physical body—something their soul saw or heard while it was separate from their body.[110] This information was later verified as true. There is no way they would have known these things unless their soul did truly leave their body for a short time."

"Wow." Zach's face was that of amazement. He was in awe.

Lucy nodded. "Wow is right. There is a lot of compelling evidence that God exists, the Bible is true, and Jesus was resurrected. But choosing to be a Christian, a follower of Jesus, still comes down to a choice, Zach. Someone can have all the evidence in the world, but they still need to choose with their heart whether to accept Jesus as their Lord and Savior."

"I'm ready," Zach said.

"What do you mean?" Lucy wasn't expecting that from Zach. He surprised her. She had a suspicion what he meant but wanted him to confirm it.

"I'm ready," Zach repeated. "To be a Christian, a follower of Jesus. I believe it's the truth. I want to be in heaven with Grandpa, and you and Dad. And Jesus. I mean it, Mom. I'm ready."

Lucy could tell from the look in Zach's eyes that he was sincere. They had talked a lot about what she believed as well as why she believed it was the truth. But she never pushed him. She knew he would have to make that decision when he was ready. She tried to hold back her emotions, but a tear trickled out along with a smile.

"Okay," she said, wiping her face and gathering her emotions.

"What do I do?" he asked.

"You don't need to do anything to earn salvation. It's a gift. You just accept it. Let's say a prayer together."

Lucy placed her hand on Zach's shoulder and led him in a prayer that he repeated after her.

"Dear God, I believe You exist. I thank You for creating me. I thank You for loving me. I admit that I'm a sinner. I need Jesus as my Savior to take away my sins. I accept Jesus as my Savior and as my Lord. Jesus, please guide me to do Your will. Amen."

Lucy opened her eyes to see Zach's head leaning over his folded hands. He then raised his head, opened his eyes, and smiled.

Lucy smiled back and then gave him a big hug. After a long embrace, she grabbed his face with both hands and kissed his forehead.

"Love you, my little bear." It was the term of endearment she had always said to him.

"I'm not tired anymore," Zach stated. "What else can we talk about?"

"Oh no. It's time for bed. Getting late. We have a big day tomorrow."

"But how did you get home from Brazil?" Zach asked, clearly trying to find something else to talk about. "You never finished the story."

"Well, the house we had seen over the bridge had a lot of good supplies. It provided what we needed to survive, and eventually we made our way home," Lucy said in a tone intended to end the conversation.

Zach clearly wasn't satisfied. "But what happened next? I need more details than that," he persisted.

"It's very late. Not tonight," Lucy said, shaking her head and standing up. "Time for you to get sleep. Like I said, we have a big day tomorrow."

"Aww. Come on," Zach pleaded. "Please, Mom."

Lucy tucked in the blankets and kissed Zach's forehead again, "That's a story for another time. We've had enough excitement for one night. You learned about your grandpa. And then made the most important decision of your life."

CONCLUSION

What do we fear? *What should we fear?*

Fear is a powerful emotion. It has a major impact on our lives—sometimes consuming our thoughts and affecting our actions. It can paralyze us. It may cause us to flee. It may motivate us to fight. We are all unique in what causes us fear and how we react.

Some fears are beneficial for keeping us safe. They serve as a warning sign to stay away from potential danger, like a child being afraid of a hot stove or a young teenager steering clear of the wrong crowd. Dangerous situations, such as a tornado, may cause us to flee. In the story, Jack, Lucy, and Peter ran from a tsunami. Jack swam feverishly away from a shark. Peter ran from an aggressive spider. When it comes to safety, fear is a good thing.

There is another way fear can be beneficial. It can sometimes motivate us to accomplish great achievements—stretch us in ways we did not know we were capable. Fear of failure may drive a sports player to perform at a higher level. Fear of death may enable some people to go to extraordinary lengths to survive—similar to Jack and his children.

But some fears are a detriment. They are an obstacle we need to overcome to do what is right or reach our full potential. Fear of embarrassment. Fear of failure. Fear of the unknown. They should not be the primary reasons that hold us back from doing what is right. These kinds of fears vary greatly by individual. Many people are terrified to speak in public and will avoid it at all costs. Some people are afraid of the doctor or needles and may avoid medical care unless absolutely necessary. Some are afraid of bees and will avoid the outdoors. There are many other examples, but I'm not trying to minimize our individual fears, nor am I suggesting we disregard danger. We should always seek to make prudent decisions. But obviously we should strive to not let fear rule our lives or become a hindrance to being the best we can be.

Jack, Lucy, and Peter encountered terrifying situations, most of which would have struck fear in any rational person. The story included what are considered to be several of the top fears: snakes, disease, plane crash, drowning, sharks, spiders, darkness, bats, claustrophobia, and heights. Which one would have been most terrifying for you? I am not sure which would have been the worst for me. Probably the plane crash or being in the water with sharks, but I am also not fond of claustrophobia or heights, so those would also be in the running.

Most of the situations in the story would give anyone tremendous fear and for good reason. However, *what should we fear the most*? Consider the words of Jesus:

> Do not be afraid of those who kill the body but cannot kill the soul. Rather, be afraid of the One who can destroy both soul and body in hell. (Matthew 10:28 NIV)

Jesus told His disciples not to be afraid of those who can kill the body, but to fear the One who determines the destination of the soul. Jesus's point is obvious—*what matters most is eternity, so ultimately the One we should fear is God*.

Someone may ask, isn't God love? The answer is yes; see the verse below from the first letter of John:

> The one who does not love does not know God, because *God is love.* (1 John 4:8 HCSB, emphasis added)

But does that mean that God's only attribute is love? Not at all. God is also holy and just. The Bible is clear about judgment for humans: some will go to eternal punishment and some will go to eternal life:

> The one who believes in the Son has eternal life, but the one who refuses to believe in the Son will not see life; instead, the wrath of God remains on him. (John 3:36 HCSB)

> "Then they will go away to eternal punishment, but the righteous to eternal life." (Matthew 25:46 NIV)

Nobody is morally perfect compared to God's standard. We will all stand before God and give an account for our lives. Contrary to what many people believe, our good deeds do *not* negate the sins we have committed. We all fall short of God's perfect moral standard. Consider the words of the apostle Paul in the Bible:

> for all have sinned and fall short of the glory of God. (Romans 3:23 NIV)

We are all guilty of sinning—rebelling against God's moral standard. Again, good deeds we have done don't negate the bad deeds (sins) we have done. This would be similar to breaking the law and being found guilty by a judge. Regardless of any good things we have done in life, we would be punished for the law we broke.

What is the punishment for breaking God's perfect moral standard? Separation from God's holiness and love—which is hell.

In the story, Jack told Lucy that *his one fear, is to fear the One*—the One who created us, the One who judges us, and the One who determines our eternal destiny. Eternal punishment should be our biggest fear, by far. It is obvious why. Eternity is without question much longer than any pain and suffering we may endure on Earth.

What do we do?

First, we should desire to pursue God. For some it can begin with fearing God and the eternal judgment we face. Fear of God recognizes that God is sovereign (God is in control of the universe, which belongs to Him), and fear helps prioritize God's rules over our desires. Do we fear spiders, sharks, and heights? Sure. We are afraid of being harmed. But shouldn't we fear our eternal destiny much more? Contrary to current thinking, we don't get to decide what is true about God and life after death based on personal preference. There is one truth about God, and the evidence is compelling that God exists and came to earth in the form of a man—Jesus.

Admittedly fear is not a necessary first step for everyone. Some people naturally desire to follow God. Obviously that path also works.

But for some people, this first step can be difficult. Evidence can help break down intellectual barriers, but this decision also requires a step forward with the heart. We need to desire a relationship with God more than just choosing to chase the joys of life. For those struggling to take this step, they should reach out to God in prayer, admitting their challenges and asking for help. There is no specific formula. *The important point is to truly seek God.*

Second, we should admit that we are sinners, that we have broken God's moral rules, and we should ask God for forgiveness. According to the Bible, it is by Jesus's sacrifice, the shedding of innocent blood by God Himself, that our sins can be forgiven. By confessing that Jesus is Lord and accepting Him as our Savior, we are saved from punishment. His sacrifice becomes the substitute for the punishment we deserve. This truth is from the Bible:

> If you declare with your mouth, "Jesus is Lord," and believe in your heart that God raised him from the dead, you will be saved. For it is with your heart that you believe and are justified, and it is with your

mouth that you profess your faith and are saved. (Romans 10:9–10 NIV)

This salvation cannot be earned by doing good deeds. The apostle Paul makes this clear in one of his letters in the Bible:

"For it is by grace you have been saved, through faith—and this is not from yourselves, it is the gift of God— not by works, so that no one can boast" (Ephesians 2:8–9 NIV)

Doing good deeds is important as a response to following the Lord, but it is not a means to salvation.

For those who claim to be Christian, but are not truly committed to the Lord, Jesus provided a stern warning:

"Not everyone who says to me, 'Lord, Lord,' will enter the kingdom of heaven, but only the one who does the will of my Father who is in heaven. Many will say to me on that day, 'Lord, Lord, did we not prophesy in your name and in your name drive out demons and in your name perform many miracles?' Then I will tell them plainly, 'I never knew you. Away from me, you evildoers!'" (Matthew 7:21–23 NIV)

Third, we should work at strengthening our relationship with God by reading the Bible, praying, and doing God's will for our life as well as worshiping God and having fellowship with other Christians at a good church.

Most of us usually don't always remember to live our life with an eternal perspective in mind. We are worried about life on earth, because that is what we currently see, but unfortunately, death will come for us all, and our eternal fate is at stake. Eternity—just let that word sink in.

You might think you are all set. You may believe you have lived a relatively good life (or maybe you haven't). Perhaps you have decided what you believe about God and heaven and you will be just fine. *But just because you have decided what you believe about religion, does that make it true?*

Contrary to current thinking, not all religions lead to heaven. It may be considered polite to say that all religions are different paths to heaven, but that is logically impossible. Different religions have fundamental beliefs that contradict; consequently, they cannot all be true. Since it is logically impossible for all religions to be true, it is inaccurate to hold this view. It may be politically correct, but it is *not loving* to say it to others. Moreover, the Bible is very clear that Jesus claimed to be the only way to heaven. Below is one Bible verse that makes this point, directly from Jesus's words:

> Jesus told him, "I am the way, the truth, and the life. *No one comes to the Father except through Me.*" (John 14:6 HCSB, emphasis added)

You may still desire to follow a different path, choosing to follow a religion or worldview that you prefer, not wishing to follow Jesus. *But when you die, will your preference be reality? Will you wish you had considered the evidence and made an informed decision about God?*

I want to be very clear that *my intention is not to be disrespectful or insulting.* I respect everyone's free will to choose what he or she believes. However, I want to share evidence and reasons I have learned and believe are critical in deciding your eternal destination. I hope you will consider them in your spiritual journey.

Jack's discussions with his daughter provided some of the real evidence and reasons that support Christianity being true. Below is a quick summary of the evidence:

1. **Beginning of the Universe**: This is a powerful argument for the existence of God. It is based on the scientific law of cause and effect—basically anything that has a beginning needs a cause, including the universe. Let's summarize the argument.

   a. The universe had a beginning (literally space, time, and matter came into existence).

   b. Since the universe had a beginning, something must have caused it to come into existence. It cannot pop into existence by itself.

   c. Since the universe consists of space, time, and matter, the cause of these elements must be spaceless, timeless, and immaterial.

   d. Moreover, creating something from nothing implies that the cause has unimaginable power.

   e. Last, the cause is very likely personal. Why? Since the cause exists infinitely, a decision must have been made at some point to create our finite universe. Only personal beings with minds make decisions.

   f. A skeptic may suggest that this argument is attempting to insert God because we don't know what else could be the cause (a god-of-gaps approach). But this is *not* the case; we are not basing this conclusion on what we don't know but rather what we *do know.*

   g. Since the cause is spaceless, timeless, immaterial, powerful, and personal, God is the best explanation.

   h. **Illustration from the story:** Picture a house, perhaps your home. Did it pop into existence without a cause? Obviously not. We live in a *building* that was caused by carpenters, an electrician, a plumber, etc. Likewise, we live in a universe that must have been caused—and the uncaused Creator is God.

Summary: The universe cannot create itself. Whoever caused it is beyond it (God).

2. **Design in the Universe**: Design is another powerful argument that God exists. This is because design is about organizing components in a certain way for a specific purpose. Purpose requires intention; intention requires an intelligent being. The natural world is filled with examples of design, which provides evidence for God. There are a variety of design arguments, but the story included two approachses: design of the universe and Earth to support the existence of life as well as information in life. Below is a summary of these points:

   a. The universe and Earth have parameters that are fine-tuned to be able to support life.
      i. Examples for the universe include gravity and the strong nuclear force.
      ii. Examples for Earth include rotation speed and distance from the sun.
   b. The fact that there are numerous parameters required for the universe and Earth to support life and the value of each parameter is extremely precise, make the likelihood of them occurring by chance mathematically impossible.

c. The existence of these parameters at extremely precise values (order) to enable the existence of life (purpose) strongly imply design, which requires intelligence and intention.

d. Atheism's counter is desperate and not supported by evidence; the multiverse theory claims that there are an infinite number of universes with different parameters and our universe happens to have just the right parameters to support life. There is no way to verify this speculation, and it shows just how powerful the evidence is for fine-tuning. Why not admit that fine-tuning implies design?

e. The design argument can also be based on the information that is in the DNA of living things. Information requires a sender with a purpose. It requires intention. Moreover, there is far too much information in the DNA of living organisms for it to have occurred by chance. This point strongly implies an intelligent designer.

f. Overall, a reasonable explanation for the design of the universe and information in our DNA is a divine intellect—God.

g. **Illustration from the story:** *Airplanes* are fine-tuned for a purpose—to fly. The universe and Earth are fine-tuned to be able to support life.

h. **Illustration from the story:** *Cell phones* are clearly designed, both in terms of their physical structure as well as the coded information needed for it to function. This same concept applies to the cells in our body, as they are extraordinarily complex physically and contain lots of information (DNA). Just as cell phones are clearly made by intelligent people, the same principle applies to our bodily cells, which require an intelligent Creator.

Summary: The universe and natural world are filled with design—and design requires intelligence (God).

1. **Existence of Morality**: This is a third powerful argument that God exists. It basically argues that the best explanation for the existence of morality is a source outside of humankind. This is because morality is not subjective (comes from the subject—human being) instead it is objective (an independent standard that exists beyond the opinions of people). Let's summarize the thinking:

   a. There is a standard for right and wrong behavior that exists. Every rational person recognizes this, especially when they are treated unfairly.

      i. Lucy recognized this when the skipper threatened her family and stole their food. The skipper's actions were wrong regardless of his opinion.

   b. Is morality simply a feeling inside of us or perhaps rules that society has decided to create? Neither.

   c. This is because certain actions themselves are wrong independent of the opinions of people or societies. We also know this because we recognize that societies can either make moral progress, move closer to a standard of goodness, or morally regress, move away from a standard of goodness.

      i. Examples of good actions are sharing, helping, and loving.

      ii. Examples of bad actions are murder, theft, and slavery.

   d. Consequently, moral rules exist beyond people, and therefore, they require an independent, transcendent source.

   e. The perfect moral character of God provides the moral standard that is both independent from the opinions of people, while still making it applicable to all humankind.

   f. Another approach to the moral argument is moral values. We recognize that people are more valuable than other aspects of nature. This does not make sense if people are simply an accident of nature—a random assortment of atoms. Rather this makes sense from a biblical perspective because we are made in the image of God.

g. **Illustration from the story:** *Music* is subjective, based on personal preference. However, morality is objective, a standard of right and wrong not based on personal preference (morality is more like *mathematics*). We may not like other people's music, but we generally don't tell them it is wrong; however, we do tell people when they are acting wrong. Since morality is objective, it must have a source outside of people—God.

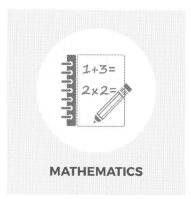

MATHEMATICS

Summary: Certain actions are right or wrong regardless of people's opinion—so the source of morality must be outside of humankind (God).

2. **Evil:** The existence of evil, which causes pain and suffering, is considered the biggest objection to the existence of God. The challenge is to understand the reasons why an all-powerful and all-good God would allow evil to exist in the world.

   There are good intellectual answers, but first it is important to recognize that they are not intended for someone who is suffering emotionally. Anyone who is suffering emotionally should be supported emotionally, not with intellectual reasons.

   Also, before we consider the intellectual response, let's look at this from a different perspective. The existence of evil actually supports an objective moral standard; in other words, there are certain actions that are evil, independent of the opinions of people. Consequently the existence of evil supports the moral argument for God (point number three above).

   That said, there are good reasons why God allows evil to exist. See below:

   a. Evil as well as pain and suffering obviously exist.

   b. There are two types of evil: moral evil and natural evil. Moral evil comes from decisions made by personal agents to commit evil acts (e.g., theft, murder), while natural evil is pain and suffering that comes from causes not related to personal decisions (e.g., disease, natural disasters).

   c. What worldview provides the best explanation? Every religion and worldview must provide an adequate explanation for evil, not just Christianity.

d. If someone is suffering emotionally, the reasons below will likely sound uncaring. They are not intended to appeal to the heart (emotional pain) but rather provide a response to the intellectual problem of evil. In other words, the reasons below are for someone who is trying to understand how both God and evil exist.

e. Reason one is free will. God has provided humankind with free will, the ability to follow God or rebel. To have true love with His creation, God provided a genuine ability to choose good or evil. Consequently free will also makes moral evil possible. The picture below illustrates free will, a person's ability to make a choice between different options:

f. Reason two is good eternal reasons. God may allow evil or pain and suffering to occur if it may benefit eternity. For example, suppose that a certain case of suffering will lead to someone seeking God and eventually going to heaven; this is clearly a good eternal reason. The challenge is we may never know what the potential good reason is, as it could be for the person experiencing the pain or someone else. God's ultimate purpose is eternity, not happiness on Earth. According to Clay Jones, Christian apologist, teacher, and author, one good reason why God allows evil is to prepare people for God's kingdom by understanding the horror of rebelling against God as well as learning to overcome evil with good.[111] The picture below is an example of God allowing an evil act (crucifixion) for an eternal good purpose (enables humankind, through faith in Jesus, to have victory over death[112]):

3. **Near-Death Experiences (NDEs):** Thousands of people have reported having a near-death experience. This is an out-of-body experience where the soul leaves the physical body for a period of time, but then returns. The experience may be on earth, in a spiritual dimension or a combination of both.[113] We need to be careful not to discern theological truth from someone's interpretation of their NDE.[114] However, NDEs do provide evidence that there truly is life after death. The following points are reasons to believe NDEs are true:

   a. Thousands of people have provided testimonies, and the descriptions of their experiences are very similar.[115]

   b. Children and people who were born blind also give similar testimonies.[116]

   c. There is no adequate natural explanation for certain NDE testimonies that provide accurate information about something they observed far away from their physical body during the NDE.[117]

4. **Bible**: Christians consider the Bible to be the inspired Word of God. It is God's special revelation to humankind, describing why our relationship with our Creator is broken and how to reconcile with God and go to heaven. The points below summarize why the Bible is a reliable source for truth as well as divinely inspired:

   a. The Bible is historically reliable. Although we don't have the original documents, we can be confident that we have the original content the authors wrote because of numerous and early manuscripts (copies).

   b. Moreover, we can believe the authors told the truth because the accounts in the Bible include numerous embarrassing details that would not have been included if they were lying.

   c. Finally, the Bible claims to be in the inspired Word of God, and we can believe this based on fulfilled prophecies.

5. **Jesus:** Jesus claimed to be God—both in His words and actions. His disciples also claimed He is God. Jesus validated this claim with evidence—miracles. This was even the form of proof He told His disciples to use if they couldn't simply accept His claim.

> "Believe Me that I am in the Father and the Father is in Me; *otherwise believe because of the works themselves.* (John 14:11 NASB, emphasis added)

But why believe the miracles actually occurred? We can believe Jesus's miracles recorded in the Bible because some include embarrassing details.

An example is the reaction of townspeople who came to meet Jesus after He healed a demon-possessed man. Rather than celebrate the miracle or glorify Jesus, they asked Him to leave their region. If the disciples were fabricating this story, it very likely would have ended differently, perhaps with Jesus being praised for the healing.

Another example is when Jesus was walking on water. Peter got out of the boat to walk to him. Peter initially believed, but then worried and began sinking. Below is Jesus' response.

Immediately Jesus reached out his hand and caught him. "You of little faith," he said, "why did you doubt?" (Matthew 14:31 NIV)

Jesus's criticism of Peter is an embarrassing detail for a key leader of the early church. It is unlikely that this would have been included if the account was a fabrication, so we have good reason to believe Jesus really did walk on water.

But the best validation for Jesus's claims is His resurrection. Based on historical evidence, the vast majority of scholars who study this topic (Christians and non-Christians) recognize that Jesus died by crucifixion, and then His disciples had experiences that they believed were with the risen Jesus. Paul, who was an enemy of Christians, converted to Christianity. James, who was Jesus's brother and a skeptic, converted to Christianity. The tomb where Jesus was laid was empty.[118] The Bible provides context for the conversions of Paul and James: Jesus appeared to them. There is no natural explanation that reasonably accounts for all of this historical data. The best explanation is that Jesus rose from the dead, validating His claim to be God, as well as providing a way for His followers to be forgiven for their sins and go to heaven.

a. **ACE**—The acronym of *ACE* is an easy way to remember the evidence for the resurrection[119]:
   i. *A*ppearances to the disciples, who were then willing to die for their claim that Jesus was resurrected
   ii. *C*onversions of Paul (previous enemy) and James (previous skeptic), who became key leaders in the early church after the resurrection
   iii. *E*mpty tomb where they had laid Jesus's body

Below is an ACE of hearts, illustrating the acronym above and God's love for humankind. There is also a picture of Jesus about to make an appearance after His resurrection.

Although there is even more evidence, the summary above provides a strong, cumulative evidential case for Christianity being true. If we choose to accept Jesus as our Lord and Savior, there is no longer any need to fear God regarding punishment. Our sins are washed away. Let me repeat that important point: if you accept Jesus as your Lord and Savior, there is no need to fear God's judgment. We can walk with God and seek to live a life of love, joy, and peace.

As Christians, we strive to live our life without being filled with anxiety or fear. Jesus said we should not worry about certain basic needs for life; rather, we should first seek the kingdom of God as this is most important.

So don't worry, saying, "What will we eat?" or "What will we drink?" or "What will we wear?" For the idolaters eagerly seek all these things, and your heavenly Father knows that you need them. But seek first the kingdom of God and His righteousness, and all these things will be provided for you. Therefore don't worry about tomorrow, because tomorrow will worry about itself. Each day has enough trouble of its own. (Matthew 6:31–34 HCSB)

Based on the verse below, we can walk with God and seek to live a life of love, joy, and peace.

But the fruit of the Spirit is love, joy, peace, patience, kindness, goodness, faithfulness, gentleness, self-control; against such things there is no law. (Galatians 5:22–23 NASB)

Also, we should have courage, not fear, in doing the will of God.

For God has not given us a spirit of timidity, but of power and love and discipline. (2 Timothy 1:7 NASB)

What role does fear play in the life of a Christian? Although Christians should not live a life of fear, it is appropriate to continue to fear God in a certain manner—out of reverence, awe, and respect. Consider the following verses in the Bible, from Proverbs and New Testament letters from the Apostles Peter and Paul:

Don't be jealous of sinners; instead, *always fear the Lord*. (Proverbs 23:17 HCSB, emphasis added)

> If you address as Father the One who impartially judges according to each one's work, *conduct yourselves in fear during the time of your stay on earth.* (1 Peter 1:17 NASB emphasis added)

> Therefore, having these promises, beloved, let us cleanse ourselves from all defilement of flesh and spirit, *perfecting holiness in the fear of God.* (2 Corinthians 7:1 NASB, emphasis added)

There is no question that life is filled with situations that bring us worry and concern. But let us *continually* remind ourselves what is most important. Based on what Jesus taught His disciples, we should fear the One who controls the destination of our soul—God. Our one fear should be to fear the One and choose our only hope for the forgiveness of our sins—accepting Jesus as our Lord and Savior.

Important Questions to Consider Regarding Your Eternal Destiny

Questions are powerful. They provide an effective way to reflect on important information. Questions are more interesting to think about than statements, which may be easier to dismiss. They can focus our reasoning process on key points to help make decisions. This chapter will offer questions for you to think about regarding the most important decision of your life: What is your belief of and commitment to Jesus?

In addition, using questions can also be a great way to share information with others in a nonaggressive manner. This can be particularly helpful with controversial topics, such as religion. It allows the other person to reflect on what is being shared. Let them consider the information, rather than be confronted with a statement that could sound aggressive or antagonistic. The best book I have read on this approach is *Tactics: A Game Plan for Discussing Your Christian Convictions*, by Greg Koukl (see the recommended reading chapter of this book). Greg's book provides some very helpful tactics to dialogue with people in an effective and respectful manner.

Below are some questions that might be helpful for you personally if you are not a Christian, but open to pursuing spiritual truth. Otherwise, if you are a Christian, the questions below may assist you in sharing your faith, provided they are asked with gentleness and respect (1 Peter 3:15). You can simply read the main questions that are in number format, or also some of the more detailed sub-questions in letter format. General comments are provided as bullets marked with arrowheads.

Is the truth about God worth your considering?

1. Will you die some day?
   - ➤ Of course (unless Jesus returns before your death). This is intended to be an obvious answer, so we can start from a point of certainty.
2. If there is life after death, would it be longer than your life on earth?
   - ➤ Again, another obvious answer. If there is life after death, it is a virtual certainty that it is longer than our relatively short lives on earth.
3. Since it is a certainty that you will die someday (#1) and life after physical death is longer than life on earth (#2), isn't the truth of God and heaven worth considering?
   - ➤ This is an obvious conclusion. Unfortunately, many people take for granted life after death. They don't consider the enormity of what is at stake.
4. Is it possible that there is more than one truth about God?
   - ➤ No. Each major religion and worldview has fundamental beliefs that contradict each other (e.g., Jesus claimed to be God and the only way to salvation). Consequently, multiple truths are logically impossible.
5. If there is only one truth about God and eternity is so important, shouldn't we consider the evidence and make an informed decision?
   - ➤ Again, another obvious answer. But it is simply to stress the importance of the topic.

Does God exist?

1. "Is it more reasonable that the universe popped into existence from nothing without a cause (atheism) or that something exists beyond the universe that created it (God)?"[120]

    a. Do you believe that the universe had a beginning?
        - Virtually everyone believes it had a beginning.
        - There is strong support from science, including the second law of thermodynamics, which supports the notion that the universe is running out of usable energy.[121]
        - There are also philosophical reasons to support a beginning of the universe, but they are beyond the scope of this book.

    b. Do you believe that everything that has a beginning must have a cause?
        - This is the law of cause and effect. If something has a beginning (effect), then something must have caused it. The effect cannot cause itself.
        - In the story, the illustration of an effect was a house, which obviously was caused by people.

    c. Since the universe consists of time, space, and matter, doesn't it make sense that the cause of the universe is timeless, spaceless, and immaterial?

    d. If the cause of the universe is timeless, spaceless, and immaterial as well as very likely powerful and personal, isn't God the best explanation of these attributes?

2. "Is it more reasonable that there are an infinite number of universes and that we are extremely lucky that our planet is able to support life (atheism) or that the universe and earth were intricately designed by a divine architect (God)?"[122]

    a. Obviously if gravity did not exist, the universe would not be able to support life. So when the universe was created, what (or who) created gravity?

b. Also, who made gravity with a very precise force that allows the universe and Earth to support life?

c. There are numerous parameters of the universe and planet Earth that allow for life to exist. Is this best explained by random chance or a divine intelligence—God?

3. Is it more reasonable that information in nature (for example, the code of life that comes from DNA), can somehow happen randomly (atheism) or that a divine mind with purpose and intent included this information in creation (God)?[123]

a. Is information material or immaterial? Is it tangible?

➢ Information is not material. It is not tangible. DNA is tangible and letters are visible, but the message or code from both is itself immaterial.

b. Does information have intention? In other words, is there a purpose behind the message? Does is require intelligence?

➢ It is obvious that information requires intelligence. Letters are organized in a specific manner to convey a message.

c. Since information is immaterial and requires intelligence, isn't God the best explanation for DNA in living organisms?

4. "Is it more reasonable that moral rules are determined by people or societies (atheism) or that the standard for good and evil is objective (actions are right or wrong independent of the opinions of people) and therefore comes from a source that transcends mankind (God)?"[124]

a. Is hurting an innocent human being for fun a bad action?

➢ Of course.

b. Is it bad only because society has decided that is the case, or is the action itself wrong?

➢ I think it is obvious that the action itself is bad regardless of the opinion of humankind. Since the standard exists separate from humankind, the source of morality must be separate from humankind.

5. "Is it more reasonable that literally everything in nature is a random collection of atoms and therefore *all* has the same value or worth (atheism) or that there is a hierarchy of value in nature, with humans at the top since we are created in God's image (God)?"[125]

    a. Is a human being more valuable than a bird?

        ➤ Obviously a human being is more valuable than a bird. It is wrong to hurt either one of them for fun, but it is more wrong to hurt a human being for fun.

        ➤ Jesus confirmed that we are more valuable than animals:

        "So don't be afraid; you are worth more than many sparrows" (Matthew 10:31 NIV)

    b. If a human being is more valuable than a bird, a dog is more valuable than an ant, an ant is more valuable than a rock, then it seems to be evident that there is a hierarchy of value for things in nature. What accounts for this?

        ➤ This makes sense if there is a something that is the most valuable for all things to be measured against (e.g., God, who is loving, merciful, all-good, all-knowing, etc.). People are made in God's image.

        ➤ Atheism cannot account for this hierarchy of value or worth in nature since everything is a random collection of atoms. There is no intrinsic value for a combination of atoms.

6. "Is it more reasonable that when people report Near Death Experiences, they are simply images in the brain (atheism), or that people have had real out-of-body experiences because they have a soul created by a divine being (God)?"[126]

a. Are you aware that thousands of people have reported leaving their body during a medical emergency and saw events on Earth and/or visited a spiritual dimension?

b. How do you account for people reporting events far away from their body that were later verified as being accurate?

> "Note: Personally, I believe God is the best answer for each of these questions, but what is really powerful is that it takes only one. Conversely, for atheism to be true, it would have to explain all these questions. *What is more likely—atheism is the right answer for all, or God is the right answer for at least one? That is the power of a cumulative case.*"[127]

Who is Jesus?

1. Do you believe Jesus existed and died by crucifixion?

> The vast majority of scholars on this topic recognize this as a historical fact. Also, if Jesus were a fictional character, why would His disciples be willing to die, and what would have convinced Paul and James to convert to Christianity? Finally, even non-Christian sources, such as Tacitus, a Roman historian, referenced Jesus and His death.[128]

2. Do you believe that Jesus claimed to be God?

a. "Is it more likely that Jesus' followers lied about His claim to be God (non-Christian) or that Jesus truly claimed to be God, which led to His crucifixion (Christian)?"[129]

> According to the Bible, Jesus claimed to be God, in both His words and actions.

3. Do you believe Jesus was resurrected from the dead?

a. "Regarding the resurrection, is there a natural explanation (non-Christian) that accounts for Jesus's appearances to

His disciples, the conversions of Paul and James, and the empty tomb (ACE)—or it more reasonable that Jesus was truly resurrected (Christian)?"[130]

> Since the majority of scholars believe that Jesus's disciples had experiences they believed was the risen Jesus, Paul and James converted from nonbelief, and the tomb was empty, isn't the resurrection the most plausible conclusion?

4. "Is it more reasonable that authors of the Bible lied about certain accounts, while also including some embarrassing details (non-Christian) or that the authors recorded the truth and believers were willing to die for their claims (Christian)?"[131]

> The Bible is historically reliable and true; consequently, we can believe the accounts, including those written about Jesus.

5. "Is it more reasonable to believe that the prophecies fulfilled in the person of Jesus are an unbelievable coincidence (non-Christian) or that the Bible is divinely inspired and Jesus is the Messiah (Christian)?"[132]

Do you accept Jesus as your Lord and Savior?

1. "Do you believe you have ever done anything wrong in life?"[133]
   a. Have you ever done something you felt guilty about?
   b. Would you say you are morally perfect or you have committed a sin?
2. "Do you believe doing something wrong deserves punishment?"[134]
   a. Do you believe that justice is a good thing?
   a. Do you believe that doing wrong actions should be dismissed without consequences or that there should be punishment?

3. "Given that you have done wrong things in life and that they deserve punishment, does the possibility of being in hell for eternity concern you?"[135]

4. "Will you accept Jesus as your Savior, substituting the punishment you deserve for the price He paid with His crucifixion, and commit to Him as Lord?"[136]

   ➢ This is the most important question in life.

   ➢ Since the evidence is compelling that God exists and Christianity is true, then the greatest danger we face is eternal punishment in hell, and our only hope is to accept Jesus as our Savior.

Study Group Questions

The purpose of this section is to provide some questions for a small group discussion. Participants should read the chapter to be discussed prior to meeting as well as the questions below that correspond to the chapter. (Important: Don't read the questions below until you have read the corresponding chapter). Some chapters have more questions depending on the events of the chapter.

I recommend opening in prayer and asking God for wisdom and guidance. Feel free to contact me if there is anything I can do to be helpful (www.jasonjolinbooks.com).

Fun Starter Questions

1. What are your biggest fears (e.g., spiders, snakes, heights)?
2. Do you have a specific example of a time when you encountered one of your biggest fears? (Not a traumatic situation, but rather a typical fear, such as spiders.)
   a. How did you deal with this situation (fight or flight)?
   b. What was the outcome?

Chapter Questions

Introduction

1. What is Christian apologetics?
2. Is Christian apologetics biblical? Read 1 Peter 3:15.

a. But in your hearts revere Christ as Lord. Always be prepared to give an answer to everyone who asks you to give the reason for the hope that you have. But do this with gentleness and respect (1 Peter 3:15 NIV).

> ➤ Depending on the Bible translation being used, you probably read either the word *answer* or *defense*, in the verse, which is from the Greek word *apologia*. This verse alone supports the discipline of apologetics being biblical.

> ➤ According to this verse, Christians should be prepared to provide an answer for *why* they believe in Jesus. How would you respond to the question: "Why are you a Christian?"

3. Read 2 Corinthians 10:3–5. According to verses 4 and 5, what type of attack do Christians encounter in this description of spiritual warfare?

a. For although we are walking in the flesh, we do not wage war in a fleshly way, since the weapons of our warfare are not fleshly, but are powerful through God for the demolition of strongholds. We demolish arguments and every high-minded thing that is raised up against the knowledge of God, taking every thought captive to the obedience of Christ. (2 Corinthians 10:3-5 HCSB).

4. Read John 14:11. Is Jesus open to the use of evidence to believe in the truth of His identity?

a. Believe Me that I am in the Father and the Father is in Me. Otherwise, believe because of the works themselves. (John 14:11 HCSB).

5. Why is Christian apologetics important (in general and specifically in today's culture)?

Prologue

1. What are the key events in the prologue? Does anyone have a favorite part?
2. Who has a fear of snakes?
3. Read Genesis 3.
   a. What aspects of the prologue are similar to Genesis 3—the fall of humankind?

Chapter 1

1. What are the key events in this chapter? Does anyone have a favorite part?
2. If you were in the position of the family, would you have stayed in Brazil or gotten on the plane? Is there anything else you would you have considered doing given their situation (based on the limited information we have)?
3. In this chapter, Jack and Lucy discussed one of the major arguments for the existence of God (the beginning of the universe). In your own words, how would you summarize the evidence for God in this chapter?
4. What specific evidence in this chapter did you find most interesting or helpful?
5. Read Genesis 1:1. How does this verse relate to this argument?
   a. In the beginning God created the heavens and the earth. (Genesis 1:1 HCSB).
6. What questions do you have regarding the evidence that can be discussed as a group (or researched further)?

Chapter 2

1. What are the key events in this chapter? Does anyone have a favorite part?

2. Who has a fear of flying? Does anyone avoid flying?

3. Jack and Lucy discussed another major argument for the existence of God (design in the universe). In your own words, how would you summarize the evidence for God in this chapter?

4. What specific evidence in this chapter did you find most interesting or helpful?

5. Read Psalm 19:1–4 and Romans 1:18–20. How do these passages of scripture relate to this evidence for God?

   a. *The heavens declare the glory of God, and the sky proclaims the work of His hands.* Day after day they pour out speech; night after night they communicate knowledge. There is no speech; there are no words; their voice is not heard. *Their message has gone out to all the earth, and their words to the ends of the inhabited world.* In the heavens He has pitched a tent for the sun. (Psalm 19:1-4 HCSB, emphasis added).

   b. For God's wrath is revealed from heaven against all godlessness and unrighteousness of people who by their unrighteousness suppress the truth, since what can be known about God is evident among them, because God has shown it to them. From the creation of the world His invisible attributes, that is, His eternal power and divine nature, have been clearly seen, being understood through what He has made. As a result, people are without excuse. (Romans 1:18-20 HCSB).

6. What specific aspects of the natural world do you recognize as being clearly designed?

7. What questions do you have regarding the evidence that can be discussed as a group (or researched further)?

Chapter 3

1. What are the key events in this chapter? Does anyone have a favorite part?
2. Who has a fear of sharks? Does anyone avoid going in the ocean for a specific fear?
3. Does anyone have a fear of life in freshwater? Snapping turtles? Certain snakes that live in or travel around the water?
4. Read Proverbs 1:7. Why would fear of God be the beginning of knowledge?
    a. *The fear of the Lord is the beginning of knowledge;* fools despise wisdom and instruction. (Proverbs 1:7 HCSB, emphasis added).
5. Does anyone have any questions for the group?

Chapter 4

1. What are the key events in this chapter? Does anyone have a favorite part?
2. Jack and Lucy discussed another major argument for the existence of God (morality: moral rules and moral values). In your own words, how would you summarize the evidence for God in this chapter?
3. What specific evidence in this chapter did you find most interesting or helpful?
4. Read Romans 2:14–15. How does this passage of scripture relate to this evidence for God?
    a. So, when Gentiles, who do not have the law, instinctively do what the law demands, they are a law to themselves even though they do not have the law. *They show that the work of the law is written on their hearts.* Their consciences testify in support of this, and their competing thoughts

either accuse or excuse them (Romans 2:14-15 HCSB, emphasis added).

5. What real-life examples of moral actions can you think of that help make the point that morality is objective (perhaps recent news events)? In other words, certain actions that are clearly wrong, demonstrating that morality is not subjective.

6. What are some examples in our society (or history of our country) of moral customs changing to improve (or perhaps the opposite – worsen)? How does that demonstrate that there is a moral standard outside of the views of society?

7. What are the some of the responses that were provided regarding the question "Why does God allow evil?"

8. What questions do you have regarding the evidence that can be discussed as a group (or researched further)?

Chapter 5

1. What are the key events in this chapter? Does anyone have a favorite part?

2. Does anyone have a fear of spiders?

3. Read Proverbs 31:30. How does fear of the Lord lead to praise?
   a. Charm is deceptive, and beauty is fleeting; but a woman who fears the LORD is to be praised. (Proverbs 31:30 NIV).

4. Read Psalm 103:11. Why do you think this verse mentions God's lovingkindness being great toward those who fear Him?
   a. For as high as the heavens are above the earth, So great is *His lovingkindness toward those who fear Him*. (Psalm 103:11 NASB, emphasis added).

5. Does anyone have any questions for the group?

Chapter 6

1. What are the key events in this chapter? Does anyone have a favorite part?
2. In your own words, how would you summarize the evidence for the Bible in this chapter?
3. What evidence in this chapter did you find most interesting or helpful (the reliability and truth of the Bible as well as being divinely inspired)?
4. Read 2 Timothy 3:16. Based on this verse, how should we view the Bible? How should it impact our approach to reading the Bible?
   a. All Scripture is inspired by God and is profitable for teaching, for rebuking, for correcting, for training in righteousness, (2 Timothy 3:16 HCSB).
5. What questions do you have regarding the evidence that can be discussed as a group (or researched further)?

Chapter 7

1. What are the key events in this chapter? Does anyone have a favorite part?
2. Read John 14:27. Discuss what Jesus said about leaving His peace and how that might relate to your life.
   a. "Peace I leave with you. My peace I give to you. I do not give to you as the world gives. Your heart must not be troubled or fearful." (John 14:27 HCSB).
3. Does anyone have any questions for the group?

Chapter 8

1. What are the key events in this chapter? Does anyone have a favorite part?

2. In your own words, how would you summarize the evidence for the resurrection of Jesus?
3. What evidence in this chapter did you find most interesting or helpful?
4. Read 1 Corinthians 15:3–8. How do these scripture verses relate to ACE, the acronym used in the book regarding the evidence for Jesus's resurrection?
   a. For I passed on to you as most important what I also received: that Christ died for our sins according to the Scriptures, that He was buried, that He was raised on the third day according to the Scriptures, and that He appeared to Cephas, then to the Twelve. Then He appeared to over 500 brothers at one time, most of whom remain to the present, but some have fallen asleep. Then He appeared to James, then to all the apostles. Last of all, as to one abnormally born, He also appeared to me. (1 Corinthians 15:3-8 HCSB).
5. What is your favorite scripture verse(s) regarding the resurrection of Jesus?
6. What questions do you have regarding the evidence that can be discussed as a group (or researched further)?

Chapter 9

1. What are the key events in this chapter? Does anyone have a favorite part?
2. Read Psalm 56:3-4. Discuss any similarities between these Bible verses with what Jack mentioned to Lucy and Peter about fearing God; and also any similarities between Psalm 56:3-4 and what Jesus said in Matthew 10:28.
   a. When I am afraid, I will trust in You. In God, whose word I praise, in God I trust; I will not fear. What can man do to me? (Psalm 56:3-4 HCSB). Don't fear those who kill the body but are not able to kill the soul; rather,

fear Him who is able to destroy both soul and body in hell. (Matthew 10:28 HCSB).

3. Read Psalm 103:13–17. Why do you think the Lord has compassion on those who fear Him?

   a. As a father has compassion on his children, so *the Lord has compassion on those who fear Him.* For He knows what we are made of, remembering that we are dust. As for man, his days are like grass- he blooms like a flower of the field; when the wind passes over it, it vanishes, and its place is no longer known. But from eternity to eternity *the Lord's faithful love is toward those who fear Him,* and His righteousness toward the grandchildren. (Psalm 103:13–17 HCSB, emphasis added).

4. Does anyone have any questions for the group?

Chapter 10

1. What are the key events in this chapter? Does anyone have a favorite part?

2. Lucy and Zach discussed the evidence from near death experiences (NDEs). How can this evidence be helpful in making a case for life-after-death? Why should we be careful not to take spiritual truth from these personal accounts (interpretations of what they saw)?

3. Read Psalm 85:9. Why do you think salvation is near to those who fear God?

   a. Surely *His salvation is near to those who fear Him,* That glory may dwell in our land. (Psalm 85:9 NASB, emphasis added).

4. Does anyone have any questions for the group?

Final Questions

1. Both of Jack's kids represent different types of people who are not Christians.
   a. Lucy was antagonistic toward Christianity. She did not believe and had no problem expressing her disbelief.
   b. Peter was apathetic toward religion. He was going through the motions but was not really a believer.
2. Who do you know personally who might relate to either of these types of people (atheist vs. apathetic)?
3. Based on the reflective questions from the prior chapter of this book, which ones might be helpful in a discussion with that person?

RECOMMENDED READING— CHRISTIAN APOLOGETICS

The Bible is the authoritative source to learn spiritual truth. It is the Word of God and should be read routinely. For anyone looking for more information on Christian apologetics, this chapter provides some books and websites to consider.

I wrote another Christian apologetic book called *Ready ... Set ... God*. It uses football illustrations to share evidence for Christianity. Some of the evidence and reasons are similar to this book, but the approach is different, and it provides even more evidence and rationale for Christianity.

Additionally, there are many great resources for Christian apologetics. Below is a list of some of the resources I would recommend (some books may have a newer edition).

Primary Recommendations

- *I Don't Have Enough Faith to Be an Atheist* by Norman L. Geisler and Frank Turek (Wheaton, IL: Crossway Books, 2004).
- *The Story of Reality: How The World Began, How It Ends, and Everything Important That Happens In Between* by Gregory Koukl (Grand Rapids, MI: Zondervan, 2017).
- *Why Does God Allow Evil?: Compelling Answers for Life's Toughest Questions* by Clay Jones (Eugene, OR: Harvest House Publishers, 2017).

Bible—Apologetic Theme

- *The Apologetics Study Bible* (Nashville, TN: Holman Bible Publishers, 2007).

Tactics for Discussions with Non-Christians

- *Tactics, 10th Anniversary Edition: A Game Plan for Discussing Your Christian Convictions* by Gregory Koukl (Grand Rapids, MI: Zondervan, 2019).

Short, But Great

- *More Than a Car*penter by Josh McDowell (Carol Stream, IL: Living Books, 2005).
- *The Third Day: The Reality of the Resurrection* by Hank Hanegraaff (Nashville, TN: W Publishing Group, 2003).
- *Mere Christianity* by C.S. Lewis (New York, NY: HarperSanFrancisco, 1980).

Comprehensive Resources on Apologetics

- *The Bible's Answers to 100 of Life's Biggest Questions* by Norman L. Geisler and Jason Jimenez (Grand Rapids, MI: Baker Books, 2015).
- *Scaling the Secular City: A Defense of Christianity* by J.P. Moreland (Grand Rapids, MI: Baker Academic, 1987).
- *Reasonable Faith: Christian Truth and Apologetics* by William Lane Craig (Wheaton, IL: Crossway Books, 1984).
- O*n Guard: Defending Your Faith with Reason and Precision* by William Lane Craig (Colorado Springs, CO: David C. Cook, 2010).
- *When Skeptics Ask: A Handbook on Christian Evidences* by Norman L. Geisler and Ronald M. Brooks (Grand Rapids, MI: Baker Books, 1990).

- *evidence for God: 50 Arguments for Faith from the Bible, History, Philosophy, and Science* by William A. Dembski and Michael R. Licona (eds.) (Grand Rapids, MI: Baker Books, 2010).
- *Philosophical Foundations for a Christian Worldview* by J.P. Moreland and William Lane Craig (Downers Grove, IL: IVP Academic, 2003).

Historical Evidence Regarding Jesus, the Resurrection, and/or the Bible

- *The Case for the Resurrection of Jesus* by Gary R. Habermas and Michael R. Licona (Grand Rapids, MI: Kregel Publications, 2004).
- *The Historical Jesus: Ancient Evidence for the Life of Christ* by Gary R. Habermas (Joplin, MO: College Press Publishing Company, 1996).
- *Cold-Case Christianity: A Homicide Detective Investigates the Claims of the Gospels* by J. Warner Wallace (Colorado Springs, CO: David C. Cook, 2013).
- *The New Evidence that Demands a Verdict: Evidence I & II Fully Updated in One Volume To Answer Questions Challenging Christians in the 21st Century* by Josh McDowell (Nashville, TN: Thomas Nelson Publishers, 1999).
- *The Risen Jesus & Future Hope* by Gary R. Habermas (Lanham, MD: Rowman & Littlefield Publishers, Inc., 2003).

Near-Death Experiences

- *Imagine Heaven: Near-Death Experiences, God's Promises, and the Exhilarating Future That Awaits You* by John Burke (Grand Rapids, MI: Baker Books, 2015).

Encyclopedias on Apologetics

- *Baker Encyclopedia of Christian Apologetics* by Norman L. Geisler (Grand Rapids, MI: Baker Academic, 2006).
- *The Popular Encyclopedia of Apologetics: Surveying the Evidence for the Truth of Christianity* by Ed Hindson and Ergun Caner (General Editors) (Eugene, OR: Harvest House Publishers, 2008).
- *The Popular Handbook of Archaeology and the Bible: Discoveries That Confirm the Reliability of Scripture* by Joseph M. Holden and Norman Geisler (Eugene, OR: Harvest House Publishers, 2013).

Christian Apologetics Websites

- str.org
- coldcasechristianity.com
- crossexamined.org
- reasonablefaith.org

NOTES

Introduction

[1]   The Bible teaches that everyone has sinned—broken God's moral standard.
      "for all have sinned and fall short of the glory of God" (Romans
      3:23 NIV).

[2]   One of the fundamental laws in logic known as the "law of
      noncontradiction." Based on this law, it is impossible for claims that
      contradict to be true at the same time and in the same sense. This
      principle of logic can be found in many sources, including R. C. Sproul,
      *The Consequences of Ideas: Understanding the Concepts That Shaped Our
      World* (Wheaton, IL: Crossway Books, 2000), 41–42.

[3]   There are multiple Bible verses that support Christian apologetics being
      a biblical concept, including the following verse which is the most
      commonly cited for apologetics:
      But in your hearts revere Christ as Lord. Always be prepared to give
      an answer to everyone who asks you to give the reason for the hope that
      you have. But do this with gentleness and respect. (1 Peter 3:15 NIV)

Prologue

[4]   Tadeu is a Brazilian name that means "given of God": https://getnames.
      net/brazilian-baby-names/.

Chapter 1

[5]   Norman L. Geisler and Frank Turek, *I Don't Have Enough Faith to Be an
      Atheist* (Wheaton, IL: Crossway Books, 2004), 93.

6   Christian philosopher and author William Lane Craig quotes a couple sources regarding the point that space and time had a beginning. He quotes British physicist and author P. C. W. Davies, making the point that not only matter and energy, but also space and time had a beginning. P. C. W. Davies, "Spacetime Singularities in Cosmology," in J. T. Fraser (ed.), *The Study of Time III* (New York: Springer Verlag, 1978), 78–79. He also quotes physicists John Barrow and Frank Tipler, who make the same point in *The Anthropic Cosmological Principle* (Oxford: Clarendon Press, 1986), 442. Both of these are quoted in William Lane Craig, "The Kalam Cosmological Argument," in William Lane Craig, ed., *Philosophy of Religion: A Reader and Guide* (New Brunswick, NJ: Rutgers University Press, 2002), 102.

7   Geisler and Turek, *I Don't Have Enough Faith*, 93.

8   The point that the cause of the universe is personal comes from multiple sources.

      Greg Koukl makes the point that all causes are either personal or impersonal, respectively agent and event causes. Event causes require a prior cause to trigger them, but since these prior causes cannot go back infinitely, there must an agent cause to start the process. Since the universe came into existence out of nothing, it is more probable that it came from an agent or personal cause—God.

      "You Bet Your Life: A Simple Cash Against Atheism" (Signal Hill, CA: Stand To Reason), CD.

      https://store.str.org/ProductDetails.asp?ProductCode=CD124.

9   Christian philosopher and author J. P. Moreland makes the point that the cause of the universe is best explained by the free act of a person, since the first event is both caused and comes spontaneously from a state of no space or time. J.P. Moreland, *Scaling the Secular City: A Defense of Christianity* (Grand Rapids, MI: Baker Academic, 1987), 42.

      Christian apologists and authors Norman Geisler and Frank Turek also make the point that the cause of the universe must be personal, because the first event required a decision to create the universe from nothingness. Geisler and Turek, *I Don't Have Enough Faith*, 93, 197.

10   Geisler and Turek, *I Don't Have Enough Faith*, 93.

11   Christian apologetics is the discipline that provides a rational defense of Christianity, using reason along with various types of evidence, such as philosophy, science, and history.

[12] This line of reasoning is one approach of *The Cosmological Argument.* It has a number of variations, but overall it *reasons that God is the best explanation for the existence of the universe.*

One variation is called the KALAM cosmological argument, which uses the principle of cause and effect to reason that the universe needs a cause. This was the variation used in our story. For a comprehensive and detailed review, I would recommend William Lane Craig's book, *The KALAM Cosmological Argument* (Eugene, OR: Wipf and Stock Publishers, 1979).

Chapter 2

[13] Philosopher, mathematician, and author Dr. William Dembski makes the point that things that are designed have the attributes of being both specified and complex. He also makes the point that everything that is designed has intention.

William A. Dembski, *Intelligent Design: The Bridge Between Science & Theology* (Downers Grove, IL: IVP Academic, 1999), 245.

[14] Nancy Pearcey in *Finding Truth: 5 Principles for Unmasking Atheism, Secularlism, and Other God Substitutes* (Colorado Springs, CO: David C Cook, 2015), 25–26 cites Robin Collins, "The Teleological Argument: An Exploration of the Fine-Tuning of the Universe," in William Lane Craig and J. P. Moreland, eds., *The Blackwell Companion to Natural Theology* (Oxford: Blackwell, 2012), that if the force of gravity were smaller or larger by one part in 10^{60}, the universe would not be habitable.

[15] Hugh Ross, *The Creator and the Cosmos: How the Latest Scientific Discoveries Reveal God* (Covina, CA: RTB Press, 2018), 233.

[16] According to astronomer and author Hugh Ross, there are over a hundred parameters in the universe that require values within a narrow range to support physical life of any sort (p. 233 of book cited below). A partial list is provided in his book below and a full list is provided on his website: *reason.org/finetuning.*

Ross, *The Creator and the Cosmos: How the Latest Scientific Discoveries Reveal God*, 233–41.

[17] Dr. William Lane Craig makes the point the laws of nature have certain constants, or values within the equations. The laws of nature are distinct from these values; in other words, they could have been different.

William Lane Craig, *On Guard: Defending Your Faith with Reason and Precision* (Colorado Springs, CO: David C. Cook, 2010), 108.

[18] Christian apologist Gregory Koukl has written a book entitled, *Faith Is Not Wishing: 13 Essays for Christian Thinkers (Published by Stand to Reason, March 2011).*

[19] Christian author, Greg Koukl, suggests that a good word to describe biblical faith is *trust*.

Gregory Koukl, *The Story of Reality: How The World Began, How It Ends, and Everything Important That Happens In Between* (Grand Rapids, MI: Zondervan, 2017), 135.

The following source on systematic theology recommends the word *trust* for understanding the biblical words for *faith* and *belief*:

Wayne Grudem, *Systematic Theology: An Introduction to Biblical Doctrine* (Grand Rapids, MI: Zondervan, 1994), 710.

[20] The force of gravity alone is extremely precise to allow for life, as referenced in the source cited above by Nancy Pearcey.

[21] Geisler and Turek, *I Don't Have Enough Faith to Be an Atheist*, 105.

[22] Scientist Hugh Ross mentions that there are nearly four hundred parameters required for a planet to support life and lists 150 in the book.

Ross, *The Creator and the Cosmos*, 218, 243–66.

[23] One estimate for the maximum number of planets in the universe of 10^{22} is referenced from Hugh Ross's third expanded edition of the following book:

Hugh Ross, *The Creator and the Cosmos: How the Greatest Scientific Discoveries Of The Century Reveal God* (Colorado Springs, CO: NavPress, 2001), 198.

[24] Ross, *The Creator and the Cosmos* (fourth edition, 2018), 219.

[25] Nicholas Bakalar, *37.2 Trillion: Galaxies or Human Cells?*, The New York Times, June 19, 2015.

https://www.nytimes.com/2015/06/23/science/37-2-trillion-galaxies-or-human-cells.html

This article references a paper published in 2013 as the source of the estimate. The process for developing the estimate was by Eva Bianconi (University of Bologna in Italy) as well as some of her colleagues.

[26] Mark Eastman and Chuck Missler, *The Creator Beyond Time and Space* (Costa Mesa, CA: The Word for Today, 1996), 34–35, quotes Michael Denton, *Evolution: A Theory in Crisis* (Chevy Chase, MD: Adler & Adler, Publishers, Inc., 1986), 250, which includes a claim that tiny bacteria cells are far more complex than anything created by humankind.

27 Dr. J. C. Sanford, *Genetic Entropy & The Mystery of the Genome* (Lima, NY: Elim Publishing, 2005), 2.

28 Sanford, *Genetic Entropy & The Mystery of the Genome*, 1.

29 Stephen C. Meyer, *Signature in the Cell: DNA and the Evidence for Intelligent Design* (New York, NY: HarperOne, 2009), 12.

30 Dr. Werner Gitt's book *In the Beginning Was Information* is a great resource for explaining why God is the best explanation for information.

Specifically, Dr. Werner makes the point that information requires a sender because information comes from the will and intention of a sender.

Dr. Werner Gitt, *In the Beginning Was Information: A Scientist Explains the Incredible Design in Nature* (Green Forest, AR: Master Books, 2005), 52–53.

31 Dr. Werner Gitt makes that point that information is not material; it is beyond the property of matter. Consequently, the source of the information cannot be material processes.

Dr. Werner Gitt, *In the Beginning Was Information*, 52.

32 This type of argument is called the *teleological argument*. Telos is Greek for purpose, and the argument is based on reasoning that there is *evidence that God exists based on all the various aspects of design in the natural world.*

Chapter 4

33 I have heard Greg Koukl, president of a Christian ministry called Stand To Reason, make the point that if God does not exist, then morality must be "inside" people, which would lead to morality being subjective. But if it is "outside" us, then it is objective, existing independently from us.

Note: Weekly radio program, "Illustrations to Show That Evil Is Evidence for God", June 15, 2018 (https://www.str.org/podcasts/illustrations-show-evil-evidence-god#.W6gCpS2ZOCQ).

34 Greg Koukl, president of STR, made the point in his debate with atheist Michael Shermer that certain actions are right or wrong and that is distinct from our feelings.

https://www.str.org/articles/greg-koukl-and-michael-shermer-at-the-end-of-the-decade-of-the-new-atheists#.W6gI1C2ZOCQ.

35 This argument is called the *moral argument*. It argues that ethics, right and wrong behavior, is best explained by a source independent of humankind. This is because moral rules are objective, not subject to people's opinions.

36 C. S. Lewis discussed the point some civilizations may have different moralities; but the differences are not a total difference. In other words, they are not completely different, such as one society deeming selfishness to be a good thing.

C. S. Lewis, *Mere Christianity* (New York: NY: HarperSanFrancisco, 2001), 5–6.

37 Christian apologist Dr. William Lane Craig explains Euthyphro's dilemma as well as the third alternative response, which is the answer that goodness is grounded in God's nature.

https://www.reasonablefaith.org/videos/interviews-panels/what-is-the-euthyphro-dilemma-bobby-conway/.

38 Norman L. Geisler, Frank Turek, *I Don't Have Enough Faith to Be an Atheist* (Wheaton, IL: Crossway Books, 2004), 179. The authors make the point that since societies can either get better morally or worse morally, the standard of morality must exist independent of society.

39 Norman Geisler and Frank Turek make the point that if God stopped all evil, God would essentially be removing free will from humankind.

Geisler and Turek, *I Don't Have Enough Faith to Be an Atheist*, 389–90.

40 Norman Geisler and Ronald Brooks make the point that God will not force people to love Him but rather provides a choice.

Norman L. Geisler and Ronald M. Brooks, *When Skeptics Ask: A Handbook On Christian Evidences*, (Grand Rapids, MI: Baker Books, 1990), 72–73.

41 Kevin Lewis, "Theological Anthropology: Essential Christian Doctrine Syllabus—Summer 2012," Biola University, 1.

42 Lewis, "Theological Anthropology," 1.

43 Christian apologist William Lane Craig defines moral duties (I am using the word *rule* in this book instead of *duty*) and moral values. Moral duties are requirements to behave in a certain manner, which determine right and wrong behavior. Moral values determine the value or worth of certain actions or people.

Craig, *On Guard*, 130.

44 Lewis, "Theological Anthropology," 1.

45 Christian philosophers J.P. Moreland and William Lane Craig make the point that God's priority for human life is not happiness, but rather knowledge of God. Also, suffering provides an opportunity for dependency and trust in God.

J.P. Moreland and William Lane Craig, *Philosophical Foundations for a Christian Worldview* (Downers Grove, IL: IVP Academic, 2003), 544.

[46] William Lane Craig makes the point that humans are finite persons with limited knowledge and insight and suffering may appear pointless to us, while God knows all and may allow suffering to achieve certain purposes.

Craig, *On Guard*, 158.

Chapter 6

[47] This is a famous point made by C.S. Lewis. If Jesus had lied about His identity, He would not be a good moral teacher; instead He would be a liar. Alternatively if He really thought He was God, but actually was not, then He would have been a lunatic. Consequently, by making the claim to be God, Jesus either is the Lord or else was a liar or lunatic; a good moral teacher is not an option.

C.S. Lewis, *Mere Christianity* (New York: NY: HarperSanFrancisco, 2001), 52.

From my (Jason's) perspective, the resurrection evidence provides confirmation that He is Lord.

[48] Below is one account in the New Testament when Jesus claimed to be God, which is confirmed based on the high priest's accusation of blasphemy:

Then the high priest stood up before them and asked Jesus, "Are you not going to answer? What is this testimony that these men are bringing against you?" But Jesus remained silent and gave no answer. Again the high priest asked him, "Are you the Messiah, the Son of the Blessed One?" "I am," said Jesus. "And you will see the Son of Man sitting at the right hand of the Mighty One and coming on the clouds of heaven." The high priest tore his clothes. "Why do we need any more witnesses?" he asked. "You have heard the blasphemy. What do you think?" They all condemned him as worthy of death. (Mark 14:60–64 NIV)

Below is the Old Testament prophecy that Jesus referenced when He took the title "Son of Man":

In my vision at night I looked, and there before me was one like a son of man, coming with the clouds of heaven. He approached the Ancient of Days and was led into his presence. He was given authority, glory and sovereign power; all nations and peoples of every language worshiped him. His dominion is an everlasting dominion that will not pass away, and his kingdom is one that will never be destroyed. (Daniel 7:13–14 NIV)

49 Below are verses that includes Jesus's claim:

"Your father Abraham rejoiced at the thought of seeing my day; he saw it and was glad." "You are not yet fifty years old," they said to him, "and you have seen Abraham!" "Very truly I tell you," Jesus answered, "before Abraham was born, I am!" At this, they picked up stones to stone him, but Jesus hid himself, slipping away from the temple grounds. (John 8:56–59 NIV)

Below is the Old Testament verse regarding the name of God:

Moses said to God, "Suppose I go to the Israelites and say to them, 'The God of your fathers has sent me to you,' and they ask me, 'What is his name?' Then what shall I tell them?" God said to Moses, "I AM WHO I AM. This is what you are to say to the Israelites: 'I AM has sent me to you.' " (Exodus 3:13–14 NIV)

50 Below is Peter's claim that Jesus is God:

Simon Peter, a bond-servant and apostle of Jesus Christ, To those who have received a faith of the same kind as ours, by the righteousness of our *God and Savior, Jesus Christ*: (2 Peter 1:1 NASB, emphasis added)

Below is John's claim that Jesus is God, specifically when he states that the Word was God and became flesh:

In the beginning was the Word, and the Word was with God, *and the Word was God … And the Word became flesh*, and dwelt among us, and we saw His glory, glory as of the only begotten from the Father, full of grace and truth. (John 1:1,14 NASB, emphasis added)

Below is Paul's claim that Jesus is God:

Looking for the blessed hope and the appearing of the glory of our great *God and Savior, Christ Jesus.* (Titus 2:13 NASB, emphasis added)

51   In the book *I Don't Have Enough Faith to Be an Atheist,* chapter 13 provides some great examples of Jesus's claims about His identity, including His actions that imply His claim to be God (specifically for the latter, see the following source). Geisler and Turek, *I Don't Have Enough Faith*, 344–45.

52   Seeing their faith, Jesus told the paralytic, "Son, your sins are forgiven." But some of the scribes were sitting there, thinking to themselves: "Why does He speak like this? He's blaspheming! Who can forgive sins but God alone?" Right away Jesus understood in His spirit that they were reasoning like this within themselves and said to them, "Why are you reasoning these things in your hearts? Which is easier: to say to the paralytic, 'Your sins are forgiven,' or to say, 'Get up, pick up your stretcher, and walk'? But so you may know that the Son of Man has authority on earth to forgive sins," He told the paralytic, "I tell you: get up, pick up your stretcher, and go home." Immediately he got up, picked up the stretcher, and went out in front of everyone. As a result, they were all astounded and gave glory to God, saying, "We have never seen anything like this!"(Mark 2:5–12 HCSB)

53   Below are examples in the Bible of people worshiping Jesus:

Then those in the boat *worshiped Him* and said, "Truly You are the Son of God!" (Matthew 14:33 HCSB emphasis added)

Just then Jesus met them and said, "Good morning!" They came up, took hold of His feet, and *worshiped Him.* (Matthew 28:9 HCSB, emphasis added)

When they saw Him, *they worshiped*, but some doubted. (Matthew 28:17 HCSB, emphasis added)

Jesus answered, "You have seen Him; in fact, He is the One speaking with you." "I believe, Lord!" he said, and *he worshiped Him.* (John 9:37–38 HCSB, emphasis added)

54   Then Jesus told him, "Go away, Satan! For it is written: *Worship the Lord your God, and serve only Him.* " (Matthew 4:10 HCSB, emphasis added)

55   When they saw Him, *they worshiped*, but some doubted. (Matthew 28:17 HCSB, emphasis added)

56   All things were created through Him, and apart from Him not one thing was created that has been created. (John 1:3 HCSB)

57 There are 5,686 partial and complete manuscripts of the New Testament written in Greek between the second (maybe the first) and fifteenth centuries; furthermore there are thousands of manuscripts in other languages. This fact is cited in Norman L. Geisler, *Baker Encyclopedia of Christian Apologetics* (Grand Rapids, MI: Baker Academic, 2006), 532.

58 According to Timothy Jones, the vast majority of variations between manuscripts are insignificant. Most variations are related to spelling differences, the order of certain words, or the relationships between nouns and definite articles.

Timothy Paul Jones, *Misquoting Truth: A Guide to the Fallacies of Bart Ehrman's Misquoting Jesus* (Downers Grove, IL: InterVarsity Press, 2007), 43.

59 Geisler and Turek, *I Don't Have Enough Faith to Be an Atheist*, 225–26.

60 Bible: Genesis 3.

61 Bible: Genesis 9:20–21.

62 Bible: 2 Samuel 11.

63 Bible: Matthew 16:21–23. Mark 8:31–33.

64 Bible: Acts 8:1–3. Acts 9:21. Acts 22:19–20. Acts 26:10–11.

65 Christian apologists Norman Geisler and Frank Turek point out a major difference between the New Testament Christian martyrs and other martyrs dying for a cause. They may all have sincerity, but New Testament Christian martyrs also had evidence, having experienced the risen Jesus.

Geisler and Turek, *I Don't Have Enough Faith*, 294.

66 Some examples from the Bible: Acts 7:54–8:3; Acts 12:1–5; Acts 21:30–36; Acts 14:19; 2 Corinthians 11:24–27.

There are multiple accounts by early church fathers that support the fact that the apostles were willing to suffer and die for their convictions. Below are examples:

- First Clement 5:2–7: Gary R. Habermas and Michael R. Licona, *The Case for the Resurrection of Jesus* (Grand Rapids, MI: Kregel Publications, 2004), 56–57.

- Polycarp 9:1–2: http://www.earlychristianwritings.com/text/polycarp-lightfoot.html.

- Ignatius of Antioch: Gary R. Habermas, *The Historical Jesus: Ancient Evidence for the Life of Christ* (Joplin, MO: College Press, 1996), 231–32.

- Tertullian— Habermas and Licona, *The Case for the Resurrection of Jesus*, 58.

[67] Christian apologist Josh McDowell provides a good summary of this point in one of his books: *The New Evidence that Demands a Verdict* (Nashville, TN: Thomas Nelson, 1999), 4–7.

[68] Greg Koukl referred to God's plan as a rescue plan.

Gregory Koukl, *The Story of Reality: How The World Began, How It Ends, and Everything Important That Happens In Between* (Grand Rapids, MI: Zondervan, 2017), 38.

[69] J. Barton Payne, *Encyclopedia of Biblical Prophecies* (London: Hodder & Stoughton, 1973), 674–75, claims that there are 1,817 predictions, referenced by Geisler, *Baker Encyclopedia of Christian Apologetics*, 609.

[70] According to Bible prophecy scholar John Walvoord, about half of the prophecies in the Bible have been fulfilled.

John F. Walvoord, *Every Prophecy of the Bible: Clear Explanations for Uncertain Times by One of Today's Premier Prophecy Scholars* (Colorado Springs, CO: Chariot Victor Publishing, 1999), 10.

[71] As written in the Bible, God claims to be the only One who can disclose the future:

Remember the former things, those of long ago; I am God, and there is no other; I am God, and there is none like me. I make known the end from the beginning, from ancient times, what is still to come. I say, "My purpose will stand, and I will do all that I please." (Isaiah 46:9–10 NIV).

[72] Author Ralph Muncaster provided multiple reasons that confirm that the Old Testament was written before Jesus was born, including that the Tanakh (the Old Testament) was recognized and work was done to translate it into Greek.

Ralph O. Muncaster, *Examine the Evidence: Exploring the Case for Christianity* (Eugene, OR: Harvest House Publishers, 2004), 328–30.

[73] Author Ralph Muncaster selected thirty specific prophecies regarding the Messiah and estimated a probability of one person fulfilling each one by chance. He then calculated the probability of one person fulfilling *all* of them, which he calculated at one chance in 10^{110}. Essentially, it is mathematically impossible to have occurred by chance, yet Jesus fulfills all of them!

Muncaster, *Examine the Evidence: Exploring the Case for Christianity*, 353–55.

[74] But as for you, Bethlehem Ephrathah, Too little to be among the clans of Judah, From you One will go forth for Me to be ruler in Israel. His

goings forth are from long ago, From the days of eternity. (Micah 5:2 NASB)

[75] For dogs have surrounded me; A band of evildoers has encompassed me; They pierced my hands and my feet. (Psalm 22:16 NASB)

[76] According to the source below, Psalm 22 was written by David, probably about 970–1,020 years before Jesus was born.

George Knight and James Edwards, eds., *Compact Bible Handbook* (Nashville, TN: Thomas Nelson, 2004), 102.

[77] It is estimated that Psalm 22 was written between 1020–970 BC.

George Knight and James Edwards, *Compact Bible Handbook* (Nashville, TN: Thomas Nelson, 2004), 102.

It is possible that the Psalm 22 prophecy about Jesus's hands and feet being pierced was predicted before crucifixion was invented; the first recorded crucifixion that we have is about 519 BC

http://www.bible.ca/d-history-archeology-crucifixion-cross.htm (references Encyclopaedia Britannica, crucifixion)

[78] Below is one example of the prophecies regarding the genealogy of the Messiah. God tells Abraham that all people on Earth will be blessed through him, which was fulfilled in the lineage of Jesus.

I will bless those who bless you, I will curse those who treat you with contempt, and *all the peoples on earth will be blessed through you.* (Genesis 12:3 HCSB, emphasis added)

[79] Bible: Numbers 21:8–9 NIV.

[80] Jason M. Jolin, *Ready … Set … God: A Football Story That Illustrates Evidence for Christianity* (Bloomington, IN: WestBow Press, 2019), 91–92.

[81] Bible: John 3:14–15 NIV.

[82] Jolin, *Ready … Set … God*, 92.

[83] Ibid.

Chapter 8

[84] Believe Me that I am in the Father and the Father is in Me. Otherwise, believe because of the works themselves. (John 14:11 HCSB)

[85] Bible: Matthew 14:22–33. Mark 6:45–51. John 6:16–21.

[86] There are multiple accounts in the Bible of Jesus healing people. Below are just some examples:

Bible: Matthew 9:1–8. Mark 6:53–56. Luke 9:10–11. John 4:46—5:15.

87 Bible: Matthew 14:13-21. Mark 6:33-44. Luke 9:12-17. John 6:1-14.

88 Frank Turek and Norman Geisler make this point, that the creation of the universe out of nothing is the greatest miracle, so miracles of the Bible are at least possible.

Geisler and Turek, *I Don't Have Enough Faith to Be an Atheist*, 203.

89 Craig Keener has written a comprehensive, two-volume book on miracles, including evidence of modern miracles.

Craig S. Keener, *Miracles: The Credibility of the New Testament Accounts* (Grand Rapids, MI: Baker Academic, 2011).

90 This miracle account can be found in two sections of the Bible: Mark 5:1–20; Luke 8:26–39.

91 These key points are provided by Christian historical scholars and authors Gary Habermas and Mike Licona's with their 4+1 minimal facts approach regarding evidence for the resurrection of Jesus. These points are based on historical data that is well evidenced and agreed on by the majority of scholars on this topic (even skeptics). The 4+1 minimal facts approach includes the following:

1. Jesus died by crucifixion.
2. Jesus's disciples believed that He appeared to them.
3. The conversion of Paul, who was an enemy of Christians.
4. The conversion of James, who was Jesus's brother and a skeptic of Jesus's claims.
5. Jesus's tomb was found empty.

Habermas and Licona, *The Case for the Resurrection of Jesus*, 47, 75.

92 This comes from an article written in the *Journal of the American Medical Association*, which used modern medical insight to confirm the death of Jesus.

William D. Edwards, Wesley J. Gabel, and Floyd E. Hosmer, "On the Physical Death of Jesus Christ," *JAMA* 255, no. 11 (March 21, 1986): 1461.

93 This comes from an article written in the *Journal of the American Medical Association*, which used modern medical insight to support the historical record that Jesus died by crucifixion.

William D. Edwards, Wesley J. Gabel, and Floyd E. Hosmer, "On the Physical Death of Jesus Christ," *JAMA* 255, no. 11 (March 21, 1986):1462–463.

94   Dr. Habermas and Dr. Licona provide a complete response to this hypothesis. including death by asphyxiation, the spear wound to the side, Jesus's separate appearance to Paul and a critique by German scholar D.F. Strauss that the disciples would not have been convinced that Jesus was resurrected given his mutilated body.

    Habermas and Licona, *The Case for the Resurrection of Jesus*, 99–103.

95   Michael Licona, historian, author, and Christian apologist, includes a point in the article below that if Jesus somehow escaped the tomb and visited the disciples, the condition of His body would not have convinced them that He had risen from the dead.

    Michael R. Licona, "Can We Be Certain That Jesus Died on a Cross? A Look at the Ancient Practice of Crucifixion", William A. Dembski and Michael R. Licona, eds., *evidence for God: 50 Arguments for Faith from the Bible, History, Philosophy, and Science* (Grand Rapids, MI: Baker Books, 2010), 166–67.

96   Dr. Habermas and Dr. Licona provide a complete response to this hypothesis: including not explaining group hallucinations, the empty tomb, and the conversions of Paul and James.

    Habermas and Licona, *The Case for the Resurrection of Jesus*, 105–09.

97   Gary R. Habermas, *The Risen Jesus & Future Hope* (Lanham, MD: Rowman & Littlefield Publishers, Inc., 2003), 17.

98   Bible: Luke 24:30; Luke 24:41–43; John 21:12–13.

99   Bible: John 20:24–29.

100   Some examples from the Bible: Acts 7:54—8:3; Acts 12:1–5; Acts 21:30–36; Acts 14:19; 2 Corinthians 11:24–27.

    There are multiple accounts by early church fathers that support the fact that the apostles were willing to suffer and die for their convictions. Below are examples:

- First Clement 5:2–7: Habermas and Licona, *The Case for the Resurrection of Jesus*, 57.
- Polycarp 9:1–2: http://www.earlychristianwritings.com/text/polycarp-lightfoot.html.
- Ignatius of Antioch: Habermas, *The Historical Jesus: Ancient Evidence for the Life of Christ*, 231–32.
- Tertullian: Habermas and Licona, *The Case for the Resurrection of Jesus*, 58.

101   Christian apologists Norman Geisler and Frank Turek point out a major difference between the New Testament Christian martyrs and other martyrs dying for a cause. They may all have sincerity, but New

Testament Christian martyrs also had evidence, having experienced the risen Jesus.

Geisler and Turek, *I Don't Have Enough Faith*, 294.

[102] Dr. Habermas and Dr. Licona provide a complete response to this hypothesis: including the disciples were willing to die as well as the conversions to Paul and James being based on appearances.

Habermas and Licona, *The Case for the Resurrection of Jesus*, 93–96.

[103] Acts 9:1–27. Acts 22:1–21. Acts 26.

[104] "Not everyone who says to me, 'Lord, Lord,' will enter the kingdom of heaven, but only the one who does the will of my Father who is in heaven. Many will say to me on that day, 'Lord, Lord, did we not prophesy in your name and in your name drive out demons and in your name perform many miracles?' Then I will tell them plainly, 'I never knew you. Away from me, you evildoers!' (Matthew 7:21–23 NIV)

[105] "Therefore, don't be afraid of them, since there is nothing covered that won't be uncovered, and nothing hidden that won't be made known. What I tell you in the dark, speak in the light. What you hear in a whisper, proclaim on the housetops. Don't fear those who kill the body but are not able to kill the soul; rather, fear Him who is able to destroy both soul and body in hell. (Matthew 10:26–28 HCSB)

"And I say to you, My friends, don't fear those who kill the body, and after that can do nothing more. But I will show you the One to fear: Fear Him who has authority to throw [people] into hell after death. Yes, I say to you, this is the One to fear! (Luke 12:4–5 HCSB)

Chapter 10

[106] Lucy is referencing something Jesus said, which is recorded in the book of John:

"No one has greater love than this, that someone would lay down his life for his friends" (John 15:13 HCSB).

[107] J. P. Moreland, "More Evidence for Life After Death," in *The Apologetics Study Bible*, ed. Ted Cabal (Nashville, TN: Holman Bible Publishers, 2007), 1598.

[108] Jeffrey Long with Paul Perry, *Evidence of the Afterlife: The Science of Near-Death Experiences* (New York, NY: HarperOne, 2010), 44,50.

[109] Long with Perry, *Evidence of the Afterlife*, 48–49.

[110] Moreland, "More Evidence for Life After Death," *The Apologetics Study Bible*, 1598.

      Long with Perry, *Evidence of the Afterlife*, 47.

Conclusion

[111] Clay Jones, *Why Does God Allow Evil? Compelling Answers for Life's Toughest Questions* (Eugene OR: Harvest House, 2017), 208.

[112] Believer's Bible Commentary references 1 Corinthians 15:57 as a verse that is understood to mean that those who have faith in Jesus have victory over death and the grave.

      William MacDonald, *Believer's Bible Commentary: Second Edition* (Nashville, TN: Thomas Nelson, 2016), 1827.

[113] Michael B. Sabom, *Recollections of Death: A Medical Investigation* (New York, NY: Wallaby Books, 1982), 52.

[114] Moreland, "More Evidence for Life After Death," *The Apologetics Study Bible*, 1598.

[115] Long with Perry, *Evidence of the Afterlife*, 44,50.

[116] Long with Perry, *Evidence of the Afterlife*, 48–49.

[117] Moreland, "More Evidence for Life After Death," *The Apologetics Study Bible*, 1598.

      Long with Perry, *Evidence of the Afterlife*, 47.

[118] These key points are provided by Christian historical scholars and authors Gary Habermas and Mike Licona with their 4+1 minimal facts approach regarding evidence for the resurrection of Jesus. These points are based on historical data that is well evidenced and agreed on by the majority of scholars on this topic (even skeptics). The 4+1 minimal facts approach includes the following:

1.   Jesus died by crucifixion.
2.   Jesus's disciples believed that He appeared to them.
3.   The conversion of Paul, who was an enemy of Christians.
4.   The conversion of James, who was Jesus's brother and a skeptic of Jesus's claims.
5.   Jesus's tomb was found empty.

Habermas and Licona, *The Case for the Resurrection of Jesus*, 47, 75.

[119] Jolin, *Ready … Set … God*, 106.

[120] Ibid., 123.
[121] Geisler and Turek, *I Don't Have Enough Faith*, 76-78.
[122] Jolin, *Ready ... Set ... God*, 123.
[123] Ibid.
[124] Ibid.
[125] Ibid.
[126] Ibid., 124.
[127] Ibid.
[128] Habermas, *The Historical Jesus, 187-190.*
[129] Jolin, *Ready ... Set ... God*, 125.
[130] Ibid.
[131] Ibid., 124.
[132] Ibid., 124–25.
[133] Ibid., 125.
[134] Ibid.
[135] Ibid.
[136] Ibid.

Printed in the United States
By Bookmasters